Lawrence Buckley Thomas

Pedigrees of Thomas, Chew and Lawrence

the West River register and genealogical notes

Lawrence Buckley Thomas

Pedigrees of Thomas, Chew and Lawrence
the West River register and genealogical notes

ISBN/EAN: 9783337302566

Printed in Europe, USA, Canada, Australia, Japan

Cover: Foto ©Andreas Hilbeck / pixelio.de

More available books at **www.hansebooks.com**

PEDIGREES

THOMAS, CHEW, AND LAWRANCE,

A WEST RIVER REGESTER,

AND

GENEALOGICAL NOTES,

BY

REV. LAWRENCE BUCKLEY THOMAS,

Cor. Mem. Wisconsin Hist. Soc.

NEW YORK:
THOMAS WHITTAKER.
2 and 3 Bible House,
1883.

WORKS BY THE SAME AUTHOR.

Genealogical Notes, containing over 50 previously unprinted Ameri can Pedigrees. Illustrated with Views and Arms. 202 pp. Imp. 4to, cloth. Baltimore, 1877..... ....$5.00

*Genealogical Notes, PART SECOND. Containing very extensive ad- ditions. Illustrated with Coats of Arms, 17 pp. Fac-similes of Early Records, Marriage Certificates, and over 300 Autographs, 94 pp. Imp. 4to, uncut. Baltimore, 1878......................$5.00

*Ditto, both Parts in one Volume. 296 pp. Imp 4to, uncut. Baltimore, 1877–8..$10.00

The Magazine of American History says of the "NOTES,"—"Well printed and arranged in the most thorough manner, the separation by groups being admirably marked by the typography."

N. E. Historical and Genealogical Register says,—"A valuable addition to American Genealogy. Pedigrees of over fifty families, with biographical sketches of much value and interest."

The poet LONGFELLOW says,—"The volume is curious and interesting; turning over its pages is like wandering through a church-yard, and reading the inscriptions on the tombs, etc."

A Dream of Arcadia, and other Verses, with 6 Illustrations. Sq. 18mo. fine cloth. Baltimore, 1879..:........................... .....$1.00

The poet LONGFELLOW says,—"Your handsome volume has given me much pleasure, and I like particularly the gentle spirit that pervades it and the simple style in which it is written."

* To be had only of the Author.

PREFACE.

In this volume, besides completely revised pedigrees of Thomas and Chew, and a previously unprinted pedigree of Lawrance of Philadelphia, compiled by E. S. Lawrance, Esq., I have printed a large collection of Notices of the Thomas, Lawrence, and Chew families in England, drawn from a variety of sources, and representing the labor of a number of years, spent in investigating all the available sources of information in this country. I believe that I have collected everything of value in elucidating the English pedigree of those families, to be found on this side of the Ocean, and, so far as I know, in print. Though I do not expect to print any further Genealogical matter, I shall be glad to learn of any inaccuracies or deficiencies in my present work. While my authorities in this volume have been the same as in my two previous collections of Genealogy, with such additions as are herein noted, the reader will bear in mind, that to find one brief notice, there may have been many volumes examined I regret that it has been impossible for me to satisfactorily ascertain the English ancestry of the Lawrence family in particular, but I congratulate myself on having dissipated some of the mist surrounding this "vexed question" by disproving baseless assumptions made by previous writers on the subject, and even by correcting my own previous tentative work in my "Genealogical Notes." In the pedigree of the Thomas family I have done all that is possible, without a personal examination of English and Welsh Records still unprinted.

In conclusion, I must express my gratitude to Samuel Chew, Esq., of "Cliveden," Messrs. Beverly and John C. Chew, of New York City, William G. Thomas, of Yonkers, N. Y., Edward S. Lawrance, Esq , of Philadelphia, Philip Alex. Thomas, of London, Eng., and the late Thomas Chew Lewis, of New York, who have been of especial assistance to me in furnishing material for this volume ; and also to the Long Island Historical Society, and their Librarian, Mr. Hannah and his assistants, for courtesies rendered to me on more than one occasion.

LAWRENCE BUCKLEY THOMAS.

All Saints' Rectory, Pontiac, R. I.
November 4th, 1882.

ARMS OF DE ZENG.

NOTE.

The abbreviations used in this book are: ap —son of; b.—born ;
d —died; dau.—daughter; d. s. p.—died without issue; G. N.,
in the index,—"Genealogical Notes," parts one and two;
m. or md.—married; (q. v)—a reference to the index;
S. P. D.—State Papers Domestic, the series of
Calendars or abstracts of the English State
Papers published by the Government of
Great Britain; and those noted at the
beginning of the West River Regester.

Chiu

CHEW.

JOHN CHEW, said to be a cadet of the family of CHEW of Chewton, in Somersetshire, England, who was a member of the Virginia House of Assembly in 1623 as a Burgess from Jamestown, appears to have been the first of this name in America. In a land grant of the same year he is described as "John Chew, Merchant."

He is said to have come over in the "Charitie" and his wife SARAH, to have followed him in the "Sea Flower" which returned to England in 1622. He was afterward a Burgess from Hogg's Island, and was in the Assembly until 1643. JOHN and SARAH CHEW had issue: SAMUEL and JOSEPH.

JOSEPH, the second son md. Nov. 17th, 1685, in Maryland, MARY SMITH, and died in the same Province Feby. 12th, 1715-16. He is also said to have married a MISS LARKIN, of Annapolis, and to have had by her a son, LARKIN CHEW. (q. v.)

SAMUEL, eldest son of John and Sarah Chew, removed to Maryland before 1655, received large grants of land there, and settled at Herring Bay in Calvert County. He md. ANNE AYRES, a prominent member of the Society of Friends, whose business meetings were long held at her house. SAMUEL CHEW d. Mch. 15th, 1676–7, and his wife April 13th, 1695. having had issue:

i. SAMUEL b. in 1660. (q. v.)

ii. JOSEPH md. Mrs. ELIZABETH (GASSAWAY) BAT-
     TEE, and d. Feb. 11th, 1704–5; his wife d. in May
     1716, leaving issue by her second husband:

    i. JOSEPH md. ——, and had issue: Joseph, Henry
     and Eliza. JOSEPH, the eldest son, had two sons:
     Nathaniel b. in 1748, md. ——, and d. s. p.
     in 1827; and JOHN md. ——, and left surviv-
     ing issue: Nathaniel b. in 1785, md. in 1814
     ——, and d. in 1845, leaving issue: JOHN W.;
     NATHANIEL since d., and two other children, one of
     whom is d. JOHN CHEW also left three other
     sons, Robert, Walter and John, and four daughters,
     Ann, Elizabeth, Artridge and Agnes.

    ii. HENRY md. ELIZABETH ——, and had issue two
     sons: Henry, who removed to one of the lower
     counties in Maryland, and Joseph b. Aug. 24th,
     1719, resided at Deer Creek, Harford Co., Md.,
     md. in 1745 Sarah ——, and had issue:
     Elizabeth b. July 18th, 1747 md. Nov. 24th,
     1768 John Hopkins (q. v.); Susan b. December
     25th, 1749; Thomas b. June 8th, 1752, md,
     Elizabeth, dau. of William and Cassandra Morgan,
     and had issue: Edward M. d. in 1880.

iii. NATHANIEL, d. after Feb. 20th, 1695.

iv. WILLIAM md. December 20th, 1690, SIDNEY, dau. of
     Thomas and Martha Wynn, of Pennsylvania, and
     d. Feb. 28th, 1709–10, leaving issue: a son BENJAMIN
     md. in January, 1726–7, SARAH BOND, and d. in
     January, 1763, leaving issue:

i.   BENJAMIN md. ——, and had issue: Nathaniel, one
     of the first midshipmen appointed by the Amer-
     ican Congress, served with Commodore Morris,
     and, being captured by the British, was confined
     in the Jersey Prison Ship. He attained the rank
     of Captain in the Navy, md. in 1792, Margaret,
     dau. of Commodore John Rodgers, and had issue:
     John; Benjamin Franklin; Washington Pinkney
     md. January 4th, 1831, Mary Hall, and had issue:
     James White, Clerk of the United States District
     Court, Baltimore; Nathaniel and William Stokes;
     Emeline R.; Henrietta Mary md. Rev. Dr. Cyrus
     Huntington; and Elizabeth Ann.

ii. SARAH who md. a JOHNS.

iii. PHINEHAS

iv. MARY md. in 1726-7, GILBERT CROCKETT.

v.   ANN who md. Capt. ISAAC VAN BIBER.

vi. HENRIETTA md. BENJAMIN GALLOWAY.

v.   BENJAMIN b. April 13th, 1671, of whom presently.

vi. SARAH md. a BURGES.

vii. ANNE d. Jany. 28th, 1699.

viii. JOHN who d. Feby. 19th, 1696-7.

ix. CALEB who d. May 8th, 1698.

BENJAMIN, fifth child of Samuel and Anne Chew,
b. April 13th, 1671, md. Dec. 8th, 1692, ELIZABETH
BENSON, (who md. 2d Sept. 24th, 1702, RICH-
ARD BOND.) her first husband d. March 3d, 1699–
1700, having had issue:

i.   SAMUEL b. Oct. 30th, 1693, was a physician by profession,
     and Chief Justice of the three lower counties of Penn-
     sylvania, Newcastle, Kent and Sussex, now included in
     the State of Delaware. Dr. CHEW md. 1st Oct. 22d,
     1715, MARY, dau. of Samuel and Anne Galloway,
     and by her (who d. May 26th, 1734,) had issue:

     i.   SARAH b. July 23d, 1716, d. in Feby. 1716-17.

     ii. ANN b. Jany. 4th, 1718-19, d. Oct. 2d, 1723.

7

iii.   ELIZABETH b. Nov. 25th, 1720, md. in 1749, Col. EDWARD TILGHMAN, of Wye. (q. v.)

iv.   BENJAMIN b. Nov. 29th, 1722, of whom presently.

v.   ANN b. April 13th, 1725, md. SAMUEL GALLOWAY. (q. v.)

vi.   MARY b. June 27th, 1727, d. May 28th, 1728.

vii.   SAMUEL b. April 29th, 1729, d. June 28th, 1729.

viii.   SAMUEL b. August 3d, 1730, d. Nov. 3d, 1730.

ix.   HENRIETTA b. March 17th, 1731-2, d. in June, 1732.

Dr. SAMUEL CHEW md. 2d Sept. 28th, 1735, Mrs. MARY GALLOWAY, dau. of Aquila Paca, and widow of Richard Galloway, and d. June 16th, 1744, having had further issue by her:

x   SAMUEL b. Aug. 24th, 1737, for many years Attorney General of the Colony, and Judge of the Supreme Court of the State of Delaware, md. ANNA MARIA, dau. of Peregrine Frisby, and d. s. p. May 25th, 1809, at Chestertown, Md.

xi.   MARY b. Sept. 6th, 1739, d. May 1st, 1740.

xii.   JOHN b. March 21st, 1739–40, d. Dec. 15th, 1807, unmarried.

ii.   ELIZABETH b. March 13th, 1694-5, md. in 1710-11, KENSEY, son of Richard Johns. (q. v.)

iii   ANN b. Oct. 14th, 1696.

iv.   MARY b. in Dec. 1698, probably d. i.

BENJAMIN, fourth son of Dr. Samuel Chew, b. November 29th, 1722, studied law under Andrew Hamilton, of Philadelphia, and in London; was Speaker of the Lower House of the Three Lower Counties (now Delaware,) Attorney General of Pennsylvania, Jany. 14th, 1755, a member of the Provincial Council the same year, Recorder of the City of Philadelphia in 1756, which position he held for twenty years; Register General of Wills Aug. 14th, 1765, and April 29th, 1774, appointed Chief Justice of the Province of Pennsylvania. When the Revolution took place, Chief Justice Chew sympathized with the mother country, although he took no active part in the contest. In 1777 when Congress arrested a number of prominent Philadelphia Friends and banished them to Fredericksburg, Virginia, Chief Justice Chew and his friend John Penn, the Proprietary of Pennsylvania, were also put under arrest, but were allowed to retire to Mr. Chew's property, Union Forge, New Jersey, and released from arrest the next year. In 1791 Mr. Chew was appointed President of the High Court of Errors and Appeal, of the State of Pennsylvania, and retained the position until the Court was abolished in 1806. He md. 1st June 13th, 1747, **MARY**, dau. of **John and Mary Galloway**, who d. November 9th, 1755 leaving issue :

i.   **MARY** b. Mar. 10th, 1747, md. May 18th, 1768, **ALEXAN-DER**, son of **John and Elizabeth (Woodrop) Wilcocks**, of Philadelphia, and d. July 22d, 1794. He d. July 22d, 1801, aged 60, having had issue: **JOHN** b. December 25th, 1769; **MARY** b. October 5th, 1771, d. i.; **ELIZABETH** b. July 9th, 1773, d. i.; **ELIZABETH** b. August 27th, 1774, d. u., March 11th, 1864; **BENJAMIN CHEW** b. December 13th, 1776, md. **SARAH WALN; ANN** b. November 13th, 1781, md. **JOSEPH REED INGERSOLL; MARY** b. January 2d, 1784, md. **CHARLES J. INGERSOLL**; and **SAMUEL** b. March 1st, 1786, md. **HARRIET MANIGAULT**.

ii.   **ANNA MARIA** b. November 27th, 1749, d. u., in November, 1812.

iii.   **ELIZABETH** b. September 10th, 1751, md. May 26th, 1774, **EDWARD TILGHMAN,** (q. v.) and d April 4th, 1842.

iv.   **SARAH** b. November 15th, 1753, md. October 22d, 1796, **JOHN GALLOWAY.** (q. v.)

v.   **HENRIETTA** b. in Sept., 1755, buried June 15th, 1756.

9

Chief Justice CHEW md. 2d September 12th, 1757, ELIZABETH, dau. of James and Mary (Turner) Oswald, who d. in 1819. He d. January 20th, 1810, having had further issue:

vi. BENJAMIN b. September 30th, 1758, of whom presently.

vii. PEGGY OSWALD b. Dec. 17th, 1760, md. May 16th, 1787, Col. JOHN EAGER HOWARD, of Maryland, and d. May 29th, 1824, having had issue: JOHN EAGER b. June 25th, 1788, md. Dec. 20th, 1820, CORNELIA ANNABELLA READ, and d. Oct. 18th, 1822; GEORGE b. Nov. 21st, 1789, Governor of Maryland, md. Dec. 26th, 1811, PRUDENCE GOUGH RIDGELY, and d. Aug 2d, 1846; BENJAMIN CHEW b. Nov. 5th, 1791, md. Feby. 24th, 1818, JANE GRANT GILMOR; WILLLIAM b. Dec. 16th, 1793, md. April 14th, 1828, REBECCA ANN KEY, and d. Aug 25th, 1834; JULIANA ELIZABETH b. May 3d, 1796, md. Dec. 7th, 1818, JOHN McHENRY, and d. May 22d, 1821; JAMES b. Dec. 17th, 1797, md. 1st SOPHIA GOUGH RIDGELY, and 2d, CATHERINE M. ROSS; SOPHIA CATHERINE b. March 6th, 1800, md. April 7th, 1825, WILLIAM GEORGE READ; CHARLES b. April 26th, 1802, md. Nov. 9th, 1825, ELIZABETH PHŒBE, dau. of Francis Scott Key, the celebrated author of the "Star Spangled Banner," and d. June 18th, 1869; and MARY ANNE b. Feby. 16th, 1806, and d. the same year.

viii. JOSEPH b. March 9th, 1763, buried Sept. 10th, 1764.

ix. JULIANNA b. April 8th, 1765, md. April 1st, 1793, PHILIP NICKLIN, and d. Aug. 11th, 1845, he d. in Nov. 1806, having had issue: ELIZABETH b. Feby. 18th, 1794, d. in Nov., 1813; WILLIAM b. in 1796, and d. in Nov. 1811; SOPHIA CHEW b. June 25th, 1798, md. May 23d, 1816 Hon. GEORGE MIFFLIN DALLAS, U. S. Minister to the Courts of Russia and England, Secretary of State, Vice-President of the United States, etc., and d. Jan. 11th, 1869; MARIA HEN-

RIETTA b. Feby. 14th, 1800, md. June 7th, 1825, EDMUND CARMICK WATMOUGH, and d. Nov. 30th, 1864; SUSAN MARGARETTA b. in 1802, d. Dec. 21st, 1872; and JULIANA CATHERINE b. Aug. 15th, 1805, d. in Feby. 1842.

x.   HENRIETTA b. Aug. 15th, 1767, d. u. March 8th, 1848.

xi.   SOPHIA b. Nov. 13th, 1769, md. HENRY PHILIPS. (q. v.)

xii.   MARIA b. Dec. 22d, 1781, d. u. March 27th, 1840.

xiii.   HARRIET b. Oct. 22d, 1775; md. in 1800, CHARLES, only son of Charles Carroll, of Carrollton, and d. April 10th, 1861, having had issue: CHARLES b. July 19th, 1801, md. in Oct., 1825, MARY DIGGS LEE; ELIZABETH md. Dr. AARON BURR TUCKER; MARY SOPHIA md. RICHARD HENRY BAYARD; BENJAMIN CHEW d. i.; HARRIET md. Hon. JOHN LEE and LOUISA md. ISAAC RAND JACKSON.

xiv   CATHERINE b. May 3d, 1779, d. u. May 28th, 1831.

BENJAMIN, sixth child of Chief Justice Chew, b. Sept. 30th, 1758, md. Dec. 11th, 1788, KATHERINE BANNING, b. July 6th, 1770, d. in 1855; he d. April 30th, 1844, having had issue:

i.   SAMUEL b. December 8th, 1789, d. March 21st, 1795.

ii.   ELIZA b. May 4th, 1791, d. March 31st, 1795.

iii.   BENJAMIN b. Dec. 5th, 1793, md. July 11th, 1816, ELIZABETH MARGARET, dau. of Chief Justice Tilghman, who d. in June, 1817; he d. Aug. 17th, 1864, having had issue: WILLIAM TILGHMAN b. June 7th, 1817, d. April 6th, 1820.

iv.   SAMUEL b. June 19th, 1795, d. u. Aug 21st, 1841

v.   JOHN b. Jany. 23d, 1797. Midshipman U. S. N. Lost at sea in the "Epervia," in Aug. 1815.

11

vi. ELIZA MARGARETTA b. Nov. 19th, 1798, md. July 25th, 1822, Hon. JAMES MURRAY MASON, of Virginia, for many years U. S. Senator from that State, and Commissioner with John Slidell from the "Confederate States" to England, whose capture by Captain Wilkes, U. S. N., while on their voyage to that country in an English vessel, came so near causing a war between the United States and England. She d. Feb. 11th, 1874, and her husband d. April 29th, 1871, having had issue: ANNA md. JOHN AMBLER; BENJAMIN; CATHERINE md. JOHN THOMAS B. DORSEY; GEORGE; VIRGINIA; IDA; JAMES MURRAY md. — HILL; and JOHN.

vii. HENRY BANNING b. Dec. 11th, 1800, of whom presently.

viii. WILLIAM WHITE b. April 12th, 1803, Secretary of Legation to Hon. George M. Dallas, American Minister to Russia, and charge' d'affaires after Mr. Dallas' return, d. November 12th, 1851.

ix. ANNA SOPHIA PENN b. March 18th, 1805, now residing at "Cliveden" with her nephew, Mr. Samuel Chew.

x. JOSEPH TURNER b. December 12th, 1806, d. in 1835.

xi. ANTHONY BANNING b. Jan. 24th, 1809, d. in Feb. 1854.

xii. CATHERINE MARIA b. May 12th, 1811, buried Oct. 26th, 1811.

xiii. OSWALD b. May 23d, 1813, drowned while bathing in the Schuylkill River, June 8th, 1824.

HENRY BANNING, seventh child of Benjamin and Katherine Chew, b. December 11th, 1800, md. HARRIET, youngest dau. of Gen. Charles Ridgely, of Hampton, who was Governor of Maryland in 1815; she d. Oct. 20th, 1835, and he md. 2d March 10th, 1839, ELIZABETH ANN, dau. of Robert Ralston, of Philadelphia, by whom he had no issue. He d. December 12th, 1866, having had issue by his first wife:

i. CATHERINE b. April 19th, 1823, d. Feby. 24th, 1824.

ii. PRISCILLA RIDGELY b. Dec. 3d, 1824, d. Feb. 11th, 1837.

iii.   CHARLES RIDGELY b. Jany. 20th, 1827, md. Dec. 10th, 1845, HARRIET GREEN, and d. Oct. 27th, 1875, having had issue: ELIZABETH ANN b. Feb. 1st, 1847, md. Dec. 13th, 1877, J. ALEXANDER GREEN; HENRY BANNING, Jr., b. Oct. 28th, 1848; ANNE SOPHIA PENN the 2nd, b Nov. 5th, 1850, md. Oct. 14th, 1875, WILLIAM GRASON; KATHERINE b. Nov. 7th, 1852; CHARLES RIDGELY, Jr., b. Sept. 6th, 1854; BENJAMIN b. Oct. 4th, 1856; HARRIET b. Jany. 10th, 1860; and SAMUEL b. Jany. 23d, 1862, d. i.

iv.   BENJAMIN b. May 27th, 1828, d. July 20th, 1829.

v.   BENJAMIN b. June 21st, 1830.

vi.   SAMUEL b. Jany. 28th, 1832, living at "Cliveden," Germantown, Pennsylvania, the "Chew House" celebrated in the History of the American Revolution as the scene of the successful defence made by a small body of British troops Oct. 4th, 1777, which decided the battle of Germantown. The Americans were in full pursuit of the defeated British when they reached the "Chew House" into which a small party had thown themselves to protect the retreat. Gen. Knox, it is said, refused to leave a fortified place behind him, and attempting to take it, found it so well defended, that time was given the British to rally and turn their defeat into a victory. Mr. CHEW md. June 20th, 1861, MARY JOHNSON, dau. of David S. Brown, of Philadelphia, and has issue: ANNA SOPHIA PENN the 3d, b. June 17th, 1862; ELIZABETH BROWN b. November 19th, 1863; DAVID SANDS BROWN b. March 3d, 1866; SAMUEL, Jr., b. April 28th, 1871.

vii.   ACHSAH CARROLL b. Jan. 22d, 1834, d. July 12th, 1834.

viii.   HENRY BANNING b. Oct. 19th, 1835, studied medicine and was graduated at Jefferson College, Philadelphia; in 1855 appointed resident physician to the Baltimore Almshouse, where he was taken ill with Typhus fever and d. April 29th, 1855.

SAMUEL, eldest son of **Samuel and Anne (Ayres) Chew,** b. in 1660, md. 1st, April 14th, 1682, **ANNE** —— and had issue by her who d. April 8th, 1702:

i. **SAMUEL** b. May 28th, 1683, of whom presently.

ii. **ANN** b. July 2d, 1685, d. Jany. 28th, 1694–5.

iii. **JOHN** b. April 8th, 1687. (q. v.)

iv. v. **JOSEPH** and **BENJAMIN,** twins, b. April 1st, 1689, the latter d. April 18th, 1698.

vi. **NATHANIEL** b. August 5th, 1692, md. **MARY** ——, who d. August 24th, 1728; he d. Jany. 30th, 1727–8, leaving issue: **NATHANIEL, JOSEPH,** and **ANN** md. in 1727, **AQUILA JOHNS.**

vii. **JOSEPH** b. April 28th, 1696, md. **SARAH** ——, and d. in Feby. 1754, leaving issue: **THOMAS, ELIZABETH,** and **SUSANNAH.**

SAMUEL CHEW md. 2d, June 29th, 1704, **Mrs. ELIZABETH (SPARROW)** widow of **WILLIAM COALE;** she d. Feby. 27th, 1709–10, and **Mr. CHEW** d. without further issue Oct. 10th, 1718.

SAMUEL, eldest son of **Samuel and Anne (——) Chew,** b. May 28th, 1683, md. August 26th, 1703, **MARY,** dau. of **Richard and Elizabeth Harrison,** b. Dec. 31st, 1684, d. Aug. 24th, 1725; he d. Oct. 31st, 1736, having had issue:

i. **SAMUEL** md. **HENRIETTA MARIA,** dau. of Philemon Lloyd, who afterwards md. Hon. **DANIEL DULANEY, Jr.,** and had issue: **LLOYD,** killed in a duel with Rev. Bennett Allen. **SAMUEL CHEW** d. March 15th, 1736–7, having had issue: **SAMUEL,** called of "Herring Bay;" **HENRIETTA MARIA** md. **EDWARD DORSEY; PHILEMON LLOYD** and **BENNETT,** twins, the former d. s. p. in March, 1770, the latter md. **ANNA MARIA,** dau. of Edward Tilghman, and had issue: Edward, d. s. p.; **MARGARET** md. **JOHN BEALE BORDLEY.** (q. v.); **MARY** md. 1st, **WILLIAM PACA,** signer of the Declaration of Independence, and had issue: John.

ii.   ANN md. Aug. 11th, 1724, **PHILIP THOMAS.** (q. v.)

iii.   **ELIZABETH** b. October 18th, 1709, d. July 29th, 1719.

iv.   **JOHN** b. September 19th, 1711, d. March 21st, 1726-7.

v.   **MARY** b. in, 1714. md. **JOHN HEPBURN,** and d. August 10th, 1770.

vi.   **RICHARD** b. in May, 1716, of whom presently.

vii.   **FRANCIS** d. May 24th 1720.

viii. **FRANCIS** b. in 1721, md. February 26th, 1749-50 **MARY LINGAN,** who d. February 12th 1764. He d. November 11th, 1775, leaving issue: SAMUEL b. January 29th, 1755; ANN b. May 15th, 1759; and RICHARD b. October 19th, 1761.

ix.   **ELIZABETH** 2d, b. June 11th, 1725, d. June 25th, 1726.

RICHARD, third son of **Samuel** and **Mary Chew,** b. in May 1716, md. January 5th, 1749-50, **Mrs. SARAH** (Lock) **CHEW,** widow of his cousin, Samuel Chew, of John, and d. June 24th, 1769; his wife d. February 1st, 1791, aged 70 years, having had issue by her 2d husband:

i.   **MARY** b. Dec. 27th, 1750, md. 1st, Feby. 10th, 1767, **Dr. ALEXANDER HAMILTON SMITH,** and had issue: UPTON, and SARAH; md. 2d, —— **LLYLES,** and d. Nov. 23d, 1793.

ii.   Maj. **RICHARD** b. April 10th, 1753, of whom presently.

iii.   Capt. **SAMUEL** b. Dec. 9th, 1755, d. Feby. 1st, 1785.

iv.   **LOCK** b. Nov. 14th, 1757, d. s. p. Dec. 9th, 1793.

v.   **FRANCIS** b. July 10th, 1760.

vi.   **SARAH LOCK** b. Nov. 20th, 1761, md. —— **LANE.**

vii. **PHILEMON LLOYD** b. July 23d, 1765, md. Oct. 28th, 1790, ANN, dau. of William Bowie, of Prince George's County, and had issue: MARGARET BOWIE b. Sept. 17th, 1791; ELIZA b. Jan. 14th, 1793; WILLIAM BOWIE b. Sept. 27th, 1794; RICHARD b. Feby. 6th, 1796; ROBERT BOWIE b. Feby. 21st, 1797; SAMUEL b. Sept. 18th, 1798 ; WALTER BOWIE b. Nov. 29th, 1799; HENRY MORTIMER b. March 17th, 1801; JOHN b. Aug. 14th, 1802, d. Aug. 23d, same year; SARAH MARIA b. Dec. 9th, 1803 ; and ANN MARIA b. Oct. 19th, 1806.

Major RICHARD, eldest son of Richard and Sarah (Lock) Chew, b. April 10th, 1753, md. 1st, Feby. 4th, 1773, MARGARET, dau. of James John Mackall, who d. May 20th, 1779, aged 24, having had issue:

i. **RICHARD** b. Oct. 4th, 1773, of whom presently.

ii. **MARY MACKALL** b. Sept. 17th, 1776, md. —— BRINGMAN, and had issue: MARGARET md. Dr. FRY.

Major CHEW md. 2d, May 2d, 1780, FRANCES, dau. of Thomas Holland, of Calvert County, Md. She d. Sept. 26th, 1799, and her husband June 6th, 1801, having had further issue:

i. **THOMAS HOLLAND** b. Oct. 27th, 1781. See page 18.

ii. **WILLIAM HOLLAND** b. Aug. 7th, 1784, d. Sept. 11th, 1799.

iii. **SARAH** b. March 16th, 1787, d. Dec. 28th, 1790.

iv. **PHILEMON** b. Feby. 20th, 1789, md. Feby. 21st, 1813, ANN MARIA BOWIE, dau. of Gen. John Brookes, b. Nov. 17th, 1789, d. July 18th, 1862. Her husband d. Sept. 30th, 1850, having had issue:

    i. RICHARD b. March 21st, 1814, d. March 30th, 1814.

    ii. WILLIAM HOLLAND b. July 10th, 1815, d. in Mch. 1841.

iii. **MARGARET SPRIGG BOWIE** b. Jan. 3d, 1818, md. June 22d, 1843, Judge **WILLIAM HALLAM TUCK,** of Annapolis, Md., and has had issue: Maria Louisa; William Hallam, d. y.; Somerville Pinkney; Frances Chew, d. y.; and Philemon Hallam.

iv. **MARIA LOUISA** b. Jan. 14th, 1820, d. in Oct. 1836.

v. **BENJAMIN BROOKES** b. Feb. 16th, 1823, d. in 1826.

vi. **RICHARD BENJAMIN BROOKES** b. May 14th, 1828, md. Nov. 23d, 1853, **LOUISA DANGERFIELD BROOKES,** and has had issue: Eliza Dangerfield b. Nov. 4th, 1854; Philemon b. Dec. 3d, 1855, d. Dec. 10th, 1855; Anna Maria Bowie b. Nov. 22d, 1856; John Brookes b. Jan. 9th, 1859; Richard Benjamin Brookes, Jr., b. Aug. 8th, 1862; Philemon Walter b. May 26th, 1863; William Hallam Tuck b. April 7th, 1867; and Sarah Dangerfield b. Aug. 13th, 1870.

v. **SARAH LOCK** b. April 28th, 1791, d. in infancy.

vi. **FRANCES** b. April 19th, 1793.

vii. **BETTIE HOLLAND** b. Sept. 19th, 1795, d. Sept. 19th, 1797.

viii. **SAMUEL LOCK** b. July 27th, 1797, d. Feby. 12th, 1798.

ix. **BETTIE H.** 2d, b. May 15th, 1799, d. Oct. 18th, 1800.

RICHARD, eldest son of Major **Richard and Margaret (Mackall) Chew,** b. Oct. 4th, 1773, md. Dec. 20th, 1804, **ELIZABETH,** dau. of **Leonard Hollyday,** and d. June 20th, 1831, having had issue :

i. **RICHARD** b. Sept. 21st, 1805, d. s. p. Sept. 23d, 1832.

ii. **SARAH AMELIA HOLLYDAY** b. April 21st, 1807, d. unmarried.

iii. **MARGARET MACKALL** b. Feby. 1st, 1809, of whom presently.

iv. **LEONARD HOLLYDAY** b. Nov. 13th, 1810, md. **AMELIA BEALL HOLLYDAY,** and d. s. p.

17

v.   JAMES JOHN b. Feby. 20th, 1813, d. s. p. Oct. 1st, 1847.

vi.   MARIA LOUISA b. May 27th, 1815, d. in Aug. 1838.

vii.   ROBERT WILLIAM BOWIE b. March 13th, 1819, md.
May 21st, 1846, MARY VIRGINIA LEVERING,
who d. in Sept. 1863, and her husband d. s. p. in
April, 1868.

viii.   MARY ELIZABETH b. March 17th, 1820.

MARGARET MACKALL, second dau. of Richard
and Elizabeth (Hollyday) Chew, b. Feby. 1st,
1809, md. March 20th, 1831, Dr. ROBERT W.
GLASS, who, after her death, md. ISABELLA
HAMILTON, and d. Nov. 4th, 1875, having had
issue by his first wife:

i.   JOSEPH b. in 1832.

ii.   ELIZABETH C. b. Aug. 27th, 1835, md. 1st, Nov. 27th,
1856, DANIEL CARROLL DIGGS, and 2d. Oct.
13th, 1870, Dr. LLEWELLYN CROWTHER. By
her first husband she had issue: MARGARET CHEW
b. Jany. 1st, 1858; and DANIEL CARROLL b. Sept.
5th, 1859, d. Oct. 24th, 1876.

iii.   RICHARD CHEW b. in Oct. 1837, d. in the C. S. A.
Dec. 7th, 1863.

iv.   MARGARET L.

THOMAS HOLLAND, eldest son of Maj. Richard
and Frances (Holland) Chew, b. Oct. 27th, 1781,
md. 1st, ELIZABETH, dau. of Walter Smith,
of Calvert County, Md., who d. Dec. 30th, 1825,
and her husband md. 2d, Feby. 7th, 1828, MARY
DAVIS, who d. Aug. 11th, 1829, leaving an only
dau. MARY ELIZABETH F. b. Feby. 28th, 1829, md.
in 1856, FREDERICK G. SMITH, and d. in 1875,
having had issue: Philemon Chew b. in 1857; Mary
Evans b. in 1859; Walter Chew; and Susan Freeland, d. i.

18

THOMAS H. CHEW d. March 16th, 1840, having had issue by his first wife:

i. RICHARD b. Sept. 26th, 1806, d. April 19th, 1809.

ii. SUSAN SMITH b. Dec. 5th, 1807, d. Sept. 9th, 1809.

iii. FRANCES ANN b. May 2d, 1810, d. Aug. 21st, 1822.

iv. WALTER SMITH b. Aug. 13th, 1811, md. Jany. 7th, 1840, MARTHA J. REID, of Wilkinson County, Miss., and has had issue:

   i. ANN REID b. Nov. 23d, 1840.

   ii. THOMAS HOLLAND b. Jany. 29th, 1843.

   iii. PHILEMON b. in. 1845.

   iv. SARAH ELLEN b. May 17th, 1848.

   v. RICHARD FLOWER b. April 15th, 1851.

   vi. ELIZABETH SMITH b. June 14th, 1853.

   vii. JAMES REID b. Aug. 26th, 1856, d. Aug. 15th, 1869.

   viii. WILLIAM SCOTT b. Sept. 15th, 1858, d. March 23d, 1861.

   ix. FREDERICK FREELAND b. Nov. 9th, 1861, d. May 31st, 1863.

v. JOSEPH SMITH b. July 15th, 1814, d. Aug. 27th, 1822.

vi. PHILEMON b. July 2d, 1816, of whom presently.

vii. DANIEL RAWLINGS b. Nov. 25th, 1819, d. July 16th, 1820.

Dr. PHILEMON, sixth child of **Thomas H.** and **Elizabeth (Smith) Chew**, b. July 2d, 1816, md. Nov. 26th, 1839, **REBECCA CHEW FREELAND,** and has issue:

i. THOMAS HOLLAND, Jr., b. Jany. 23d, 1842.

ii. ELIZABETH b. April 12th, 1843, md. Dr. T. B. POINTDEXTER.

iii. MARIA LOUISA b. Dec. 28th, 1844, md SAMUEL G. SMITH.

iv. SUSAN HAWKINS b. April 21st, 1846.

19

v.   JOSEPH WALTER b. March 15th, 1849.

vi.   WILLIAM FREELAND b. Nov. 20th, 1851.

vii.   EDWARD b. Oct. 25th, 1855, d. in 1870.

viii.   MARY CECELIA b. March 17th, 1858, d. in 1868.

JOHN, second son of Samuel and Anne Chew, and grandson of Samuel and Anne (Ayres) Chew, b. April 8th, 1687, md. in 1708, ELIZA HARRISON, who md. 2d, in 1722, ELIHU HALL. Her first husband d. before 1718, having had issue:

i.   SAMUEL, of whom presently.

ii.   ANN md. Aug. 17th, 1727, JOSEPH, son of Gerrard and Margaret Hopkins. (q. v.)

iii.   MARY.

SAMUEL, only son of John and Eliza (Harrison) Chew, md. SARAH, dau. of Dr. Richard Lock, and d. in London in 1749, leaving issue:

i.   SAMUEL b. in 1727, of whom presently.

ii.   JOHN. (q. v.)

iii.   WILLIAM b. in 1746. (q. v.)

iv.   ELIZABETH md. 1st, —— SMITH, and 2d, —— SPRIGG.

SAMUEL, eldest son of Samuel and Sarah (Lock) Chew, b. in 1737, md. 1st, —— WEEMS, and had issue:

i.   SAMUEL, who removed to Kentucky in 1805; was in the State Legislature, and md. twice, his second wife, —— SMITH, was a sister of the wives of Thomas Holland Chew and Gen. Zachary Taylor. He d. about 1820, and is buried at St. Francisville, La., leaving issue: Dr. EDWARD d. of yellow fever about 1825; and SAMUEL, who remained in Kentucky, and had issue: Dr. Samuel.

PROFESSOR OF THE PRINCIPLES AND PRACTICE OF MEDICINE,

in the

University of Maryland.

SAMUEL CHEW md. 2d, PRISCILLA, dau. of Rev. Samuel Claggett, and descended from Col. Edward Claggett, of Canterbury, England, who md. Margaret, dau. of Sir Thomas Adams, founder of a Professorship of Arabic at the University of Cambridge. SAMUEL CHEW d. February 20th, 1790, leaving issue: JOHN HAMILTON b. September 14th, 1771, md. his cousin, PRISCILLA E., dau. of Rt. Rev. Thomas John Claggett, D. D., first Bishop of Maryland, and the first Bishop of the Protestant Episcopal Church consecrated in the United States, and d. March 22d, 1830, having had issue: MARY md. FAYETTE GIBSON; SAMUEL, of whom presently; THOMAS JOHN md. JANE BLAKE; WILLIAM PACA; PRISCILLA md. Rev. HENRY WILLIAMS; ELIZABETH; and Rev. JOHN H. md. GENEVIEVE CLAGGETT.

SAMUEL, eldest son of John Hamilton Chew, b. April 29th, 1807, was graduated at Princeton College in 1825, and in medicine, at the University of Maryland in 1829; was appointed Professor of Materia Medica in that University in 1841, and transferred to the Chair of Practice of Medicine in 1852. He md. 1st, ELIZA M. FITZHUGH, and had issue:

i.   ELIZA M.

Dr. SAMUEL CHEW md. 2d, HENRIETTA S. SCOTT, and d. December 26th, 1863, leaving further issue:

i.   ANNA.

ii. SAMUEL CLAGGETT was graduated at Princeton College in 1856, and in Medicine at the University of Maryland in 1858; was appointed to the Chair of Materia Medica and Clinics in the same University, in 1864.

iii. HENRIETTA S.

JOHN, second son of **Samuel and Sarah (Lock) Chew,** md. ——— ———, and d. May 26th, 1785, leaving issue:

i   **JOHN LANE** b. in 1762, of whom presently.

ii.   **SAMUEL** md. Nov. 1st, 1803, **ANN SMITH,** and had issue: WILLIAM PACE b. Nov. 21st, 1806; SARAH ANN b. June 21st, 1808; HORACE b. May 12th, 1812; and EDWARD R., who. d. Nov. 8th, 1829.

iii.   **NATHANIEL LANE.**

iv.   **WILLIAM LOCK** md. **REBECCA FREELAND,** who d. June 12th, 1840.

JOHN LANE, eldest son of **John Chew,** b. in 1762, md. **MARY R. WILSON,** who d. in 1802, her husband d. in 1832, having had issue:

i   **ELIZABETH** b. in 1788, d. unmarried in 1870.

ii.   **JOHN** b. Dec. 3d, 1790, of whom presently.

iii.   **EDWARD** b. in 1794, at the Old Homestead, "Lombardy Poplar," Anne Arundel County, and resided there. He md. **MARY SPARROW,** (who afterwards md. **UPTON SCOTT KEY,**) and d. leaving issue: THOMAS EDWARD b. in 1840.

JOHN, eldest son of **John Lane and Mary (Wilson) Chew,** b. Dec. 3d, 1790, entered the U. S. Navy about 1805, and served for many years, acting as Recruiting Officer in the service, with headquarters at Philadelphia and New York. He resigned in 1817, and joined the Mexican Expedition of Gen. Espoz y Mina, acting as his Chief of Staff. After the failure of that attempt he returned to the United States and entered the merchant service as captain of a vessel in the trade between Baltimore and the Mediterranean ports. Retired from the sea in 1826, removed to North Mississippi in 1835, and, engaging in cotton planting, amassed a considerable fortune. He md. May 28th, 1828, **MARY ANN SMITH,** of Calvert

County, Md., who d. July 10th, 1876, her husband d. Feby. 24th, 1872, having had issue, with seven other children who d. in infancy:

i.   GLORVINA b. May 15th, 1830, d. unmarried.

ii.   JOHN CALHOUN, b. May 28th, 1838, residing in New York City, md. 1st, July 11th, 1861, ZILPHIA GUTHRIE FULLER, and had issue: JOHN MARSHALL b. May 17th, 1862. Mrs. CHEW d. Aug. 8th, 1863, and her husband md. 2d, Feby. 1st, 1876, THEODORA R. SEIXAS.

iii. FRISBY FREELAND b. Oct. 9th, 1839, resides at Houston, Texas, md. Sept. 26th, 1861, JULIA A. FULLER, and has had issue: FREELAND FULLER b. May 22d, 1863; ROBERT EDWARD b. April 11th, 1865, d. April 25th, 1865; FRANK NATHAN b. March 19th, 1866; BEVERLY b. July 28th, 1868; MARY ANN b. May 17th, 1870; SAM YOUNG b. Jany. 25th, 1873, d. Feby. 2d, 1873; EDWARD TILGHMAN b. Sept. 3d, 1876; ZYLPHIA JULIA b. Dec. 11th, 1878, d. Dec. 27th, 1878; JOHN b. June 9th, 1880.

iv. ROBERT EDWARD b. Oct. 28th, 1844, resides at Holly Springs, Miss., md. Oct. 25th, 1865, MARY PUGH GOVAN, and has had issue: JULIA HAWKS b. June 24th, 1866; EDWARD GOVAN b. Sept. 9th, 1867; FRISBY FREELAND b. Oct. 9th, 1869; RALPH b. Sept. 27th, 1872; WILLIAM ROBERTS b. Nov. 24th, 1873, d. July 15th, 1880; FRANCIS HAWKS b. May 9th, 1875; CARRIE b. May 8th, 1877; MARY PUGH b. Oct. 26th, 1879.

WILLIAM, third son of John and Eliza (Harrison) Chew, b. in 1746, md. ELIZABETH, dau. of Thomas Reynolds, who d. April 1st, 1801. He d. April 9th, 1801, leaving issue:

i.   SARAH b. July 11th, 1770, md. 1st, ALLEN BOWIE, of Prince George's County, Md. and had issue: FIELDER; md. 2d, Dr. FRISBY FREELAND, of Mississippi; and 3d, BEVERLY R. GRAYSON, of the same State, and d. Sept. 10th, 1843.

ii.   ELIZABETH b. April 26th, 1772, md. —— MOSEBY, of Kentucky, and d. in June, 1828.

iii. FRANCES HOLLAND b. Dec. 12th, 1774, md. —— CALVIT or CALVERT, of Mississippi, and d. Aug. 24th, 1834.

iv.   MARY b. June 4th, 1776, md. Dr. THOMAS REYNOLDS, of Mississippi, and d. May 1st, 1821.

v.   WILLIAM LOCK b. April 10th, 1778, of whom presently.

vi.   ANN REYNOLDS b. July 19th, 1780, md. —— CRAIG, of Kentucky.

WILLIAM LOCK, only son of William and Elizabeth (Reynolds) Chew, b. April 10th, 1778, md. October 22d, 1805, REBECCA, dau. of Frisby and Sarah (Rolle) Freeland, b. April 30th, 1785, in Calvert County, Md., d. June 12th, 1840, in Yazoo County, Mississippi. WILLIAM L. CHEW d. July 17th, 1858, at Bay St. Louis, Mississippi, having had issue:

i.   WILLIAM b. July 12th, 1806, d. July 6th, 1807.

ii.   FRISBY FREELAND b. April 7th, 1808, md. Feb. 28th, 1837, MARIA ANGELICA, dau. of Gen. Geo. W. and Ann M. (Hopewell) Biscoe, of Washington, D. C., and d. July 11th, 1849, having had issue:

    i.   GEORGE BISCOE b. Dec. 31st, 1837, d. Aug. 18th, 1840.

    ii. WILLIAM LOCK b. Feb. 4th, 1841, d. Dec. 2d, 1864, in the C. S. A., of wounds received at the battle of Franklin, Tenn.

    iii. MONROE GRAYSON.

iv.   GEORGE BISCOE.

v.   REBECCA FREELAND md. CHARLES HUNTINGTON LYMAN, U. S. N., and has issue: Charles Huntington b. Sept. 22d, 1875; and David Hinckley b. Oct. 14th, 1877.

vi.   FIELDER BOWIE.

iii.   WILLIAM LOCK b. Feby. 2d, 1810, md. Feby. 10th, 1831, SUSAN MONROE SMITH, and d. June 8th, 1844.

iv.   FRANCES ANN b. Mar. 9th, 1812, d. Sept. 10th, 1816.

v.   SARAH ROLLE b. July 12th, 1814, md. 1st, July 8th, 1830, Major SPENCE MONROE GRAYSON, and 2d, Gen. F. T. GRAYSON; by her first husband she had issue: THOMAS THORPE b. March 16th, 1835, d. in 1876; REBECCA FREELAND; WILLIAM CHEW b. July 21st, 1837; and SPENCE MONROE.

vi.   AUGUSTIN FREELAND b. July 23d, 1816, d. July 24th 1816.

vii.   AUGUSTIN b. March 22d, 1818, md. in 1859, ELIZABETH, dau. of Col. Lewis W. Thompson, of Mississippi.

viii.   BEVERLY GRAYSON b. Jany. 21st, 1820, md. ELIZABETH, dau. of Col. Frederick Smith, of Mississippi, and had issue: FREDERICK SMITH; WILLIAM LOCK; and AUGUSTIN.

ix.   EDWARD ROBERT b. Oct. 12th, 1823, d. June 19th, 1826.

x.   THOMAS REYNOLDS b. Feb. 22d, 1826 of whom presently.

xi.   ROBERT EDWARD b. Jan. 19th, 1829, Commander of a regiment in the C. S. A., and killed at the battle of Prairie Grove, Arkansas, in 1862.

Dr. THOMAS REYNOLDS, tenth child of William and Elizabeth (Reynolds) Chew, b. February 22d, 1826, md. November 7th, 1851, MARY, dau. of Edward Butler Grayson, of Washington, D. C., and has issue: WILLIAM LOCK b. September

28th, 1855: ROBERT EDWARD; SARAH ROLLE; MARY GRAYSON; REBECCA FREELAND; SPENCE MONROVIA; BETTIE; THOMAS REYNOLDS; and EDWARD GRAYSON.

LARKIN CHEW, son of Joseph and —— (Larkin) Chew, was in Virginia before 1700; md. HANNAH, dau. of John Roy, of Port Royal, Virginia, and had issue:

i.   JOSEPH d. in infancy.

ii.   THOMAS, (q v.)

iii. ANN md. WILLIAM JOHNSTON, and had issue: JOSEPH; LARKIN md. MARY ROGERS; JUDITH md. ROBERT FARISH; ROBERT md. ANN COOK; JOHN d. unmarried; BENJAMIN md. DOROTHY JONES, and had issue: William, Gabriel, Mary Ann, Benjamin, Sirpey, and Robert; JAMES md. MARY WARE; WILLIAM md. ANN FLINT; HANNAH md. FRANCIS COLEMAN; RICHARD md. 1st, DOROTHY WALLER, dau. of William Beverly, and 2d, ANN, SMITH; and ELIZABETH md. JOHN BENGER.

iv.   JOHN, of whom presently.

v.   LARKIN. (q. v.)

JOHN, second surviving son of Larkin and Hannah (Roy) Chew, md. MARGARET, dau. of Col. Robert Beverly, Clerk of the Council of Virginia in 1679, and author of the History of Virginia, by R. B., Gent., published in 1705; and had issue:

i.   ROBERT, of whom presently.

ii.   MARY BEVERLY md. Col. JOSEPH BROCK, of Spottsylvania, Va., and had issue: JOHN md. ANN CURTIS; ELIZABETH md. 1st, J. T. LEWIS, and 2d, BEVERLY STUBBLEFIELD, or STRIBBLEFIELD; MARY md. JOHN CARTER; CATHERINE d. unmarried;

JOSEPH, a Captain in U. S. A., md. ANN, dau. of John and Ann (Fox) Chew, and had issue: Julia Ann Chew md. Silas Wood, of New York, Cadwallader William d. unmarried; Mary d. in infancy; WILLIAM md. 1st, —— BARNES, and 2d, BETSEY TOWLES: and SUSAN md. BEVERLY ROBINSON.

iii. MARGARET d. in youth.

iv. JOHN. (q. v.)

v. HANNAH md. JOHN CARTER.

ROBERT, eldest son of John and Margaret (Beverly) **Chew**, md. **MOLLY PARROTT**, of Middlesex, and had issue:

i ROBERT BEVERLY d. u.

ii. JOHN md. ELIZABETH SMITH, and had issue:

    i. ROBERT SMITH md. ELIZABETH FRENCH and had issue: John James md. Eleanor Patton, and had issue: Ann Mercer, Richard S., Eliza F. d. i., Ellen Patton, Hugh Patton, Eliza French, and Margaret H.; George French d. u.; Ann Eliza md. Lieut. George Minor, U. S. N. and had issue: John Chew; Robert Smith md. Elizabeth R. Smith, and had issue: Richard Smith md. —— Nourse, Elizabeth F. d. u., Harriet P., Robert S., John James, Louis F., Walter H., and Leonard C.

    ii. MARY BEVERLY md. SETH BARTON.

    iii. ELIZABETH md. Dr. JAMES FRENCH.

iii. HENRY d. u.

iv. ELIZABETH md. LARKIN STANARD.

v. JOSEPH, of whom presently.

JOSEPH, youngest son of Robert and Molly (Parrot) **Chew**, md. **MARY WINSLOW**, and had issue:

i. ROBERT BEVERLY d. u

ii.   JOHN WINSLOW md. ANN THORNTON VOSS, and had issue: MARY WINSLOW, of whom presently; ROBERT BEVERLY; ALEXANDER VOSS d. u. in 1851; AUGUSTA WASHINGTON d. y; JOSEPH; HENRY d. y. in 1833; ELIZABETH; THOMAS ROLLINS; JOHN d. y.; ALBERT G. md. RACHEL MURPHY and had issue: Elizabeth d. y., Mary, and Emma; FRANCIS THORNTON md. MARY W. WINSOR.

MARY W. CHEW, the oldest dau., md. J. B. TERRY, and had issue: Emelia R. md. Dr. George Buchanan; Junius Adrian d y.; Adriana md. C. W. Towner Mary W. d. y; Elizabeth R. d. u. in 1870; Josephine d. y.; Catherine; Joseph; Augusta; and Roberta Lee.

iii.   ALBERT GALLATIN md. NANNIE NORRIS, of Pennsylvania, and has issue: MARY MILLER md. G. W. E. ATKINS; and NANNIE M. N.

iv.   ADELINE W. md. 1st, JAMES VAUGHN, and had issue: JAMES ALBERT md. SALLIE LEWIS. ADELINE (CHEW) VAUGHN md. 2d, WILLIAM McCONNELL, and had issue: MARY C. md. J. W. LANCASTER.

v.   JOSEPH md. 1st, MARY LAMME, and had issue: VERNON TILFORD md. ANNA WILLIAMS; MARIA HELEN md. E. M. SLOAN; SAMUEL d. i.; JOSEPH d. u., in California, in 1864. He md. 2d, MARY BROWN, and had issue: ADELINE W. md. —— MORRIS, of Montana; THOMAS d. i.; HENRY; VIRGINIA; GEORGE d. i.; JOHN d. y.; MARY PRICE; and ROBERT LEE.

vi.   WILLIAM R. md. HELEN M. WARE, of Kentucky, and had issue: EMMA WINSLOW md. D. S. SNODGRASS; SALLIE PARRISH md. Judge M. D. ECTOR; ELLEN md. 1st, —— PINKERTON; 2d, Dr. EDWARD INGLIS; MARY ADELINE md. GEORGE A. PEETE; ANNA BEVERLY md. Dr. L. S. RAYFIELD; WILLIAM BARTLETT; JAMES EDMOND; and JOSEPH JOHNSON.

Ben Chew.

JOHN, second son of John and Margaret (Beverly) Chew, was a Colonel in the Revolutionary Army, md. in 1772, ANN, dau. of Thomas Fox, and d. in 1799; his wife d. in 1820, having had issue:

i   BEVERLY b. in 1773, of whom presently.

ii.   JOHN d. in 1838, unmarried.

iii.   PHILADELPHIA CLAIBORNE md. BROOKER WAL-LER.

iv.   ANN md. her cousin Capt. JOSEPH BROCK, U. S. A.

v.   THOMAS d. unmarried.

vi.   ELIZABETH md. ROBERT CAMMACK.

vii.   ROBERT md. LOUISE DE MARCELLON, and d. s. p.

viii.   CLAIBORNE d. unmarried.

ix.   MARY d. in 1871, unmarried.

x.   LUCY d. unmarried.

xi.   CAROLINE MATILDA md. Col. JOHN STANARD.

xii. . . MARGARET d. in infancy.

BEVERLY, eldest son of John and Ann (Fox) Chew, b. in 1773, removed to New Orleans in 1797, was Collector of the Port from 1817 to 1829, President of the Branch Bank of the United States, and Vice Consul of Russia. He md. January 14th, 1810, MARIA THEODORA DUER, dau. of Col. W. Duer, of New York City, and grand daughter of Lord Stirling, of the Revolutionary Army, and d. in 1851, having had issue:

i.   BEVERLY d. in 1828, unmarried.

ii.   CAROLINE d. in 1823, unmarried.

iii   LUCY md. WILLIAM DUER, son of Judge John Duer, of New York City.

iv.   WILLIAM.

v.   KATHERINE md. Judge THOMAS KENNEDY, and d. in 1863.

vi.   ROBERT d. in infancy.

vii.   ALEXANDER LAFAYETTE, of whom presently.

viii.   MARY VIRGINIA md. MARTIN G. KENNEDY, and d. in 1863.

ix.   MORRIS ROBINSON md. April 10th, 1860, MARY MEDORA KENNEDY, of New Orleans, La., and has had issue: MARY MEDORA b. in 1861; JOSEPH WITHERS b. in 1862; JOSEPH BEVERLY b. in 1865; MARY ROSE b. in 1868; MARY VIRGINIA b. in 1869; MORRIS ROBINSON b. in 1874, d. the same year.

ALEXANDER LAFAYETTE, seventh child of Beverly and Maria Theodora (Duer) Chew, b. Oct. 4th, 1824, md. in 1849, SARAH AUGUSTA, dau. of Phinehas Prouty, of Geneva, N. Y., and has had issue:

i.   BEVERLY b. March 5th, 1850, md. Dec. 11th, 1872, CLARISSA, dau. of Rev. Job Pierson, D. D., of Ionia, Michigan.

ii.   HARRIET HILLHOUSE b. Dec. 8th, 1851, md. in 1874, ERNEST CLEVELAND COX, son of Rt. Rev. A. Cleveland Coxe, Bishop of Western New York, and has issue: ARTHUR CLEVELAND b. in April, 1876.

iii.   PHINEAS PROUTY, b. Feb. 1st, 1854, md. Oct. 15th, 1879, MARGUERITE, dau. of Philip Pistor, of New York, and has issue: THEODORA MARGUERITE b. Aug. 28th, 1880.

iv.   THOMAS HILLHOUSE b. May 26th, 1856.

v.   ALEXANDER DUER b. Sept. 21st, 1858.

vi.   KATE ADELAIDE b. April 17th, 1861.

vii.   THEODORA AUGUSTA b. Feb. 12th, 1863, d. in 1874.

viii.   LILLIAN BEVERLY b. Feb. 19th, 1866.

LARKIN, fifth child of **Larkin** and **Hannah** (Roy) **Chew,** md. **MARY BEVERLY,** and had issue:

i. ELIZA BEVERLY md. 1st, **BEVERLY STANARD,** and 2d, **MOSES BUCKNER.** By her first husband she had issue:

    i. WILLIAM md. BELLA CARTER.

    ii. LARKIN, of whom presently.

ii. MARY md. 1st, **JOHN SMITH,** and had issue: LARKIN; and 2d, **OLIVER TOWLES,** of Caroline Co., Va.

LARKIN, second son of **Beverly** and **Eliza** (Chew) **Stanard,** md. **ELIZABETH,** only dau. of **Robért** and **Molly** (Parrot) **Chew,** and had issue:

i. BEVERLY CHEW md. MARY B. FLEMING.

ii. Judge ROBERT resided at Richmond, Va., md. JANE CRAIG.

iii. MARY B. md. EDMUND FOSTER.

iv. Col. JOHN md. CAROLINE MATILDA, dau. of John and Ann (Fox) Chew,

v. THOMAS md —— PENNY, of Louisiana.

vi. HUGH md. Mrs. ANN SIMPSON.

vii. ELIZABETH md Dr. WOOLDRIDGE.

viii. KITTY md. CHRISTOPHER BRANCH, and d. in 1822.

ix. LAVINIA d. unmarried.

x. CAROLINE MATILDA CHEW md. EATON STANARD.

xi. COLUMBIA md. —— PRATT.

xii. LUCY ANN d. in infancy.

THOMAS, eldest surviving son of **Larkin** and **Hannah (Roy) Chew,** md. **MARTHA,** dau. of **Col. James Taylor,** of York River, Va., and sister of President Madison's grand-mother, Mrs. Ambrose Madison, and had issue:

i.   JOSEPH md. GRACE DESHON, of New London, Conn., and had issue:

    i.   JOSEPH d. u. in Jamaica.

    ii   WILLIAM JOHNSTON, a British officer, killed at Niagara.

    iii.   JOHN d. u. at Montreal.

    iv.   FRANCES md. GABRIEL SISTARE, and d. in 1820, having had issue: Joseph md. Mary Christophers, and had issue: Charles md. —— Bassett, and has issue.

    v.   GRACE d. u. at Montreal.

ii.   LARKIN d. u. in Virginia, in 1796.

iii   FRANCES md. HENRY DOWNS, of Va.

iv.   HANNAH d. u.

v.   THOMAS d. y.

vi.   COLEBY, d. u. at Fort Du Quesne, in 1758.

vii.   ELIZABETH d. u.

vi.i.   ALICE md. her cousin, ZACHARY TAYLOR, of Virginia, grandfather of President Taylor, and d. in 1796.

ix.   MILDRED md. —— COLEMAN, and d. s. p.

x.   SAMUEL, of whom presently.

xi.   JAMES md. in 1765, MARY CALDWELL, of Virginia.

SAMUEL, fifth son of **Thomas** and **Martha (Taylor) Chew,** was an officer in the American Navy, d. in active service in 1779. He md. **LUCY MILLER,** of New Haven, Conn., and had issue:

i   COLEBY, of whom presently

ii.   SAMUEL, q. v.

iii.   **THOMAS JOHN** b. in 1771, entered the U. S. Navy in 1799, and was Lieutenant of the "Chesapeake" in her fight with the "Shannon," and Capt. James Lawrence, when mortally wounded and supported in his arms, gave him his dying command: ' Don't give up the ship." He resigned from the Navy in 1832; md. Sept. 10th, 1812, **ABBY HORTENSE HALLAM,** and d. in 1846, having had issue:

i.   JAMES LAWRENCE b. April 3rd. 1814, d. u. Oct. 22d, 1829.

ii.   BETSEY PRENTIS b. April 19th, 1816, d. May 11th, 1816

iii.   ELIZABETH HALLAM.

iv.   LUCY b. Dec. 13th, 1820, d. Jan. 8th, 1821.

v.   ABBY HORTENSE md. Sept. 15th, 1842, McREE SWIFT, of Geneva, N. Y., and has had issue: Hortense Hallam d.; Louisa Walker; Elizabeth Chew md. George H. Janeway, of New Brunswick, N. J.; Alexander Joseph; Lawrence Chew; Thomas Delano; Jonathan Williams d.; Josephine Richards; Robert Hallam d.; and Mary Lewis.

vi.   MARY HALLAM md. April 15th, 1844, GEORGE RICHARDS LEWIS, of New London, Conn., and has had issue: Harriet Richards md. Francesco Barbiellini, Conte d' Amidei of Rome, Italy, and has issue: Elizabetta; Hortense md. Rev. Henry Wells Nelson, Jr., of Boston, Mass., and has issue: Margaret, Howard, George Lewis, Frank Howard, and Mary Hallam Chew; Thomas Chew; Mary Elizabeth.

vii.   LUCY CHRISTOPHERS md. Sept. 30th, 1848, M. LUDLOW WHITLOCK, of New York City, and has had issue: Frank Wallace md. Oct. 4th, 1876, Zella A. Kempton, of West Newton, Mass., and has issue: Pauline; Edward Hallam d. i.; Edward Bull d. y.; and Lewis Norman d. y.

COLEBY, eldest son of **Samuel** and **Lucy (Miller) Chew,** md. **FRANCES LEARNED,** of New London, Conn., who d. in 1846. He d. in 1803, leaving issue:

i.   **FRANCES** b. in 1800, md. **LEONARD COIT,** of New London, Conn., and d. in 1866, having had issue:

    i.   FRANK d. u.

    ii.   HORACE md. Feb. 8th, 1870, EMILY, dau. of Coleby and Mary C. (Law) Chew. She d. in 1881, having had issue: Coleby Chew; Fanny Learned; Frank; and James Lawrence.

    iii.   FANNY d. y.

ii.   **COLEBY** b. in 1802, md. Oct. 10th, 1832, **MARY CECELIA LAW,** of New London, Conn., and d. in 1852, having had issue:

    i.   MARY CECELIA md. October 21st, 1852, WILLIAM CLEVELAND CRUMP, of New London, Conn., and has had issue: Eliza Richards; and John Guy md. Aug. 28th, 1878, Jennie Elizabeth Williams, of New London, Conn., and has issue: William Cleveland.

    ii.   FRANCES d. y.

    iii.   COLEBY d. y.

    iv.   RICHARD d. i.

    v.   ALICE.

    vi.   JAMES LAWRENCE.

    vii.   EMILY md. her cousin, HORACE COIT.

    viii   JULIA BEVERLY d. u.

SAMUEL, second son of **Samuel** and **Lucy (Miller) Chew,** md. **MARY SABIN,** of New London, Conn., and d. in 1834. She d. in 1855, having had issue:

GENEALOGICAL NOTES.

i. **LUCY** md. **JAMES MORGAN SMITH**, of Georgia, and d. s. p.

ii. **SAMUEL COLEBY** d. in 1832.

iii. **THOMAS JOHN** md. ———, no issue; lives in Iowa.

iv. **ANTHONY SANDFORD** md. 1st, **ELIZABETH VAN VECHTEN**, of New York City, and had issue: **ELIZABETH** md. **DUDLEY FAY**. Mr. **CHEW** md. 2d, **DELIA ADAMS**, of Columbus, Ohio, and has further issue: **THOMAS** md. **CATHERINE FORBES**, of Brooklyn, N. Y.; **DELIA** md. **JOHN BROWN**; and **DEMAS**.

v. **MARY SABIN** md. Dr. **J. N. KEELER**, of New Jersey, and has issue: **LUCY**; and **COLEBY**.

vi. **JAMES SMITH** md. **ELIZABETH KIRK**, of Ohio, who d. s. p.

35

LAWRENCE.

BY EDWARD SHINN LAWRANCE, ESQ.

The name *Laurence* as applied to men, is of very early origin. The *orthography* of the word has been slightly varied in its common usage, yet the number of syllables, it is believed, has never been changed; nor the essential vowel and consonant sounds altered. Dissyllabic, with an *a* and either a single or double *u* in the first syllable, the second has always had for its vowel short *a*, or *e*, followed by *ns*, or *nce*.

If not in its application to the same person, as used in the same family for several successive generations it has been found written in at least three, if not four various, yet similar ways; namely: *Laurens, Laurence, Lawrence*, and LAWRANCE.

Its derivation we trace to the Latin *Laurus-Laurentius*. The latter form is that in which the name is found as first given to men. The signification of the word recorded by some one (not an indifferent scholar) on the first page of the Town Records, of Hingham, Mass., may be regarded as pretty near the truth:

"Christian names for men now most used with the signification *Laurence*, flourishing like a Bay tree."

The *source* of the word is the *Laurus nobilis*, or true laurel, which is a native of Italy, and grows in the South of Europe and Asia, and in the North of Africa. By the Romans it was consecrated to Apollo, and used to decorate the brows of victors.

The very first application of the name to any one of the human family, found on record, was to ACCA LAURENTIA, the nurse of Romulus and Remus. This was more than seven hundred and fifty years before Christ.

The *Laurentalia* feasts, celebrated among the Romans on the tenth of the kalends of January, or 23d of December, were in memory of ACCA LAURENTIA, wife of the shepherd Faustulus, and nurse of Romulus and Remus. ACCA LAURENTIA, from whom the solemnity took its name, is represented as no less remarkable for the beauty of her person, than her lasciviousness; on account of which she was nick-named, by her neighbors, *lupa*, the she-wolf; which has given rise to the tradition of Romulus and Remus being suckled by a wolf. She afterward married a very rich man, who brought her great wealth, which, at her death, she left to the Roman people; in consideration whereof they performed these honors to her memory.

The man who *immortalized* the name, was LAWRENCE, of Rome, A. D. 258. He was Archdeacon of St. Sixtus, Bishop of Rome. It was ascertained that Lawrence was the keeper of the treasure of the church, and he was arrested and ordered to produce it. He asked a day in which to collect it. All night he hurried about Rome, in and out of its poorest streets and courts; on the morrow he appeared before the Court, followed by a crowd of the poor, the halt, and the blind; said he: "These are the treasures of the Church." He was ordered to death, by cruel torture. He was to be broiled on a gridiron, over a slow fire; the fire was made ready; he was stripped and laid on the iron bars; but he seemed insensible to the torture; he said, with a playful smile, to his tormentors: "Turn me, I am roasted on one side." The man who had the courage to say, "Turn me, I am roasted on one side;" and the charity to say, of the poor, the halt and the blind, "These are the treasures of the Church;" was indeed fit to be canonized as St. Lawrence.

About A. D. 250, there was another distinguished Laurence. In the persecution of Decius, he was brought before Tiburtius, the Governor at Arretium, the modern Arezzo; after severely reprimanding him, as he was of noble birth, the Governor dismissed him, strictly enjoining him, as he valued his life, not to labor to convert others to his superstition, as he called the religion of Christ. As, however, he refused obedience, he ordered him to be decapitated. He also was canonized St. Laurence.

A. D., 576, St. Laurence, the Illuminator, is said to have come from Syria, with many other illustrious bishops, to Italy, in the reign of Diocletian. He was elected by the clergy, Bishop of Spoleto, and illumined his diocese with his teachings and miracles.

The first instance of an individual to whom the name belonged who lived in England, was Laurence, Archbishop of Canterbury, A. D., 619. Laurence was one of the first missionaries to the Saxons, who came over with St. Augustine, and he succeeded the Roman Apostle of England in the See of Canterbury, in 608, in which he sat eleven years. In the reign of King Eadbald, Archbishop Laurence died, and was buried in the Church of St. Peter, close beside his predecessor Augustine.

It is, however, to ROBERT LAWRENCE, of Lancashire, we are to look for the first individual of the name, whose family and circumstances entitle him to be considered the ancestor of the LAWRENCES of England.

Born, probably, as early as A. D., 1150, he accompanied his Sovereign, Richard Cœur de Lion, to the war of the Crusades, in the Holy Land, and so distinguished himself in the siege of Acre that he was knighted Sir Robert of Ashton Hall, and obtained for his Arms, "Arg. a cross raguly Gu." A. D., 1191.

LAWRANCE
Of Philadelphia.

In "A Display of Heraldry," in England, the LAW-RANCES are emblazoned as follows:

LAWRANCE, [Foxcot, in Gloucestershire].

Ar. a cross raguly gu.—Crest, a wolf's head Ar. charged on the neck with a cross croslet gu.

LAWRANCE, [Foxhall, in Gloucestershire].

Ar. a cross raguly gu. in the first quarter a lion passant of the last.—Crest, a wolf's head proper, charged on the neck with a crescent or.

LAWRANCE, [Hampshire].

Ar. a cross betw. four cinquefoils gu.—Crest, on a chapeau gu. turned up erm. a talbot sejant gu.

LAWRENCE, [Chelsea in Middlesex, of Delaford and Chertsey in Buckinghamshire, and of St. Ive's in Huntingdonshire].

Ar. a cross raguly gu. on a chief az. three leopard's heads or.—Crest, a demi-turbot erect gu. the tail upwards.

These arms *Argent* a Cross raguly *Gules*, on a Chief
Azure, three leopards heads *Or.* are borne by the name of
Lawrance or *Lawrence*, and was given by *William De-
thick* Garter, Anno Domini, 1594, to . . . LAWRANCE,
of London, Goldsmith.

Goldsmiths in England, were Bankers. The company
received their first charter in 1327, and are still entrust-
ed with the assaying and stamping of all gold and silver
plate manufactured in London. It is understood to be
the oldest Guild in the world.

———

"Sn't Sepulchre's,
LONDON.*

"RICHARD LAWRANCE was buried in Chick Lane
"Burial Ground, from Smithfield, on the 4th day of
"June, 1737."

"August 15th, 1740.
"MARGARET LAWRANCE, widow, buried in Sn't
"Giles' Cripplegate."†

"*Extracts from the Register Book of this Parish,*
November 17th, 1789."
"*per* WM. SALMER,
"*Register Keeper.*"

———

*This Church was built in the reign of Henry VI, or Edward IV.
The bell is tolled when an execution takes place in Newgate.

†This Church was built in 1545, after a fire. In it lie the mortal re-
mains of Milton. Portions of the ancient Roman wall may be seen in the
Cemetery.

41

THOMAS LAWRANCE, son of Richard and Margaret Lawrance, was born in LONDON, A. D. 1707, and died in the Province of New Jersey, September 4th, 1775.

Very early he bore his testimony to the calming influence and seasoning virtue of Truth, and became a member in unity with the Society of Friends.

This action so disturbed the concord existing between him and his family, that he resolved to go to the Colonies in America.

He was thoroughly educated, being a master of the Latin and Higher Mathematics.

He married **SUSANNA VAN EMAN**, a daughter of **David Van Eman, Esquire**, and **Eleoner**, his wife.

She was born, Anno Domini, 1718, and died on the 21st of May, 1790.

They had children as follows:

1. DAVID LAWRANCE, b. 7th mo. 21st, 1739.

2. ELIZABETH LAWRANCE, b. 12th mo. 25th, 1740-1.

3. THOMAS LAWRANCE, b. 1st mo. 7th, 1742-3.

4. JOSIAH LAWRANCE, b. 6th mo. 14th, 1745.

5. JESSE LAWRANCE, b. 8th mo. 7th, 1747, and departed this life the 9th mo. 27th, 1749.

6. RICHARD LAWRANCE, b. 8th mo. 16th, 1749.

7. JASON LAWRANCE, b. 5th mo. 3d, 1751.

8. ISAAC LAWRANCE, b. 9th mo. 30th, 1753, N. S., and departed this life the 10th mo. 23d, 1753.

9. SAMUEL LAWRANCE, b. 11th mo. 2d, 1755,

10. MARY LAWRANCE, b. 5th mo. 16th, 1758.

1.   DAVID LAWRANCE, son of Thomas and Susanna (Van Eman) Lawrance, d. July 15th, 1799, unmarried and intestate. His Brother Thomas was his administrator. His estate was divided among his next of kin: his brothers Thomas, Richard, and Samuel, his sister Mary, his nieces Amy Fenimore, Susanna Folwell, and Elizabeth Gardiner, and Thomas Lawrance, guardian of Jason O'Brien Lawrance, his nephew.

2.   ELIZABETH LAWRANCE, daughter of Thomas and Susanna (Van Eman) Lawrance, m. JOHN GARDINER about 1770, and d. Nov. 28th, 1775. They had children :

AMY b. June 24th, 1773, m. JOHN FENIMORE about 1793.

SUSANNA b. Sept. 19th, 1774, m. JOHN FOLWELL on April 14th, 1796.

ELIZABETH b. Nov. 17th, 1775, m. her first cousin, JOHN LAWRANCE, on the 23d of Sept. 1811. She died Feb. 7th, 1833. See their children presently.

3.   THOMAS LAWRANCE, (of Philadelphia,) son of Thomas and Susanna (Van Eman) Lawrance, of Springfield Township, Province of New Jersey, m. HANNAH HALLOWELL, daughter of John and Hannah Hallowell, in Friends' Meeting, at Philadelphia, 5th mo. 12th, 1768.

Witnesses : John Hallowell, Mary Hallowell, Thomas Hallowell, Elizabeth Lawrance, Jason Lawrance, Samuel Lewis, Sarah Lewis, and 47 others.

HANNAH . (Hallowell) LAWRANCE, wife of THOMAS LAWRANCE, was born 24th of 12th mo. 1745, d. 3d mo. 1771, her age being 25 years, 3 mo. 5 days.

THOMAS and HANNAH (Hallowell) LAW-
RANCE had one child only:

JOHN b. 14th of 4th mo., 1769, died 7th mo. 26th, 1770,
aged 15 months.

HANNAH (Hallowell) LAWRANCE was an aunt
of Judge JOHN HALLOWELL, of Philadelphia, and a
grand-aunt of Mrs. STROUD, widow of Judge GEORGE
M. STROUD, of Philadelphia.

THOMAS LAWRANCE was married again about
12th mo., 1773, to ANN PALMER.

In the record of burials, kept by Friends' Meeting,
at 15th and Race streets, Philadelphia, appears:

"10th mo. 5th, 1778, ELIZABETH LAWRANCE, daughter
"of THOMAS LAWRANCE, aged 3 months.
"9th mo. 7th, 1778, A SON of THOMAS LAWRANCE,
"aged about 5 months.
"7th mo. 14th, 1780, MARY LAWRANCE, daughter of
THOMAS."

THOMAS and ANN (Palmer) LAWRANCE had
three other children:

JOHN; THOMAS; and SAMUEL.

JOHN LAWRANCE, son of Thomas and Ann
(Palmer) Lawrance, b. June 12th, 1775, m. his first
cousin, ELIZABETH GARDINER, Sept. 23d, 1811,
and died Feb. 5th, 1834.

His will is on record at Mount Holly, New Jersey,
dated 9th Sept., 1833. Executors: Peter De Cou, of Springfield, and his kinsman, Jason Lawrance Fenimore, of Philadelphia. His estate was large. Beneficiaries: His house-
keeper, Mary Mount, a faithful friend of the family; his
niece, Eliza Gardiner Lawrance; and the rest and remainder of his estate to his only child, ELIZABETH
GARDINER LAWRANCE. "But in the event that my said

daughter Elizabeth should decease before she arrives at lawful age to dispose of said real estate, by will or otherwise, and without lawful issue, it then is my will that the said real estate shall go to the surviving children of my brother Samuel Lawrance, share and share alike."

JOHN and ELIZABETH (Gardiner) LAWRANCE had two children only: JOHN GARDINER b. June 29th, 1814, d. June 6th, 1815, aged 11 mo. 8 days. ELIZABETH GARDINER b. July 12th, 1816, d. Sept. 19th, 1841; testate and unmarried, aged 25 years, 2 mo., 7 days.

Her will is on record at Mount Holly, New Jersey, dated 5th October, 1839. Executors: William Lippincott and Joseph E. Butterworth, of Springfield. Her estate was large. Beneficiaries: To Mary Mount, the faithful friend who had been house-keeper for her father, and mother, and herself, she gave the right to live and remain in the house in which she resided, with use of furniture and appurtenances, during her life; also an annuity; at her death, the principal to go to the surviving children of her uncle, Samuel Lawrance; also, *fire-bote* off of her woodlands. To her aunt Hannah Lawrance, an annuity. To her friend Elizabeth R. Hill, a legacy. Her aunt Susan Folwell, a legacy, and grand-mother's gold sleeve buttons; her silver sugar tongs; mother's silver shoe buckles and the remainder of mother's wearing apparel. Her aunt Amy Fenimore, a legacy. Her cousin Hettie G. Fenimore, a legacy, and silver cream cup marked "E. L.," and silver soup ladle with same initials. Her cousins Ann Folwell, Susan Folwell, and Elizabeth Folwell, each a legacy. Her cousin Ann Stokes, a legacy. Her cousin Mary Lawrance, a legacy. Her cousin Edward S. Lawrance, a legacy. Her cousins, *once removed*, John F. Bryan and William H. Bryan, each a legacy. Her cousin Eliza G. Lawrance, the principal of the annuity left to her mother, Hannah Lawrance, after her death, gold watch and chain, large walnut bureau, wearing apparel, piano, silver sugar bowl and cream cup, marked "E. G. L.," double hair mattrass, bedstead and bed and curtains in front room, the best carpet and rug belonging to the parlor, the large gilt-frame looking glass and mahogany breakfast table, the desk and papers in it, carriage, harness, saddle and bridle, and horse now in possession of Joel Mount; also, the residue and remainder of the estate, both real and personal, or whatsoever nature it may be, including the dwelling house, garden, stables and furniture belonging thereto, after the death of Mary Mount.

THOMAS LAWRANCE, son of Thomas and Ann (Palmer) Lawrance, m. ELIZABETH, daughter of Thomas Barnes, a merchant of Philadelphia. She was a sister of Dr. John Barnes, of Philadelphia. They had no children. He died in Philadelphia, 8th mo. 30th, 1811, leaving his wife a widow, and she married again.

His will is on record at Philadelphia, dated 18th August, 1811; proved, 5th Sept., 1811. Executors: His wife, Elizabeth Lawrance, and his father-in-law, Thomas Barnes. The estate was large. Beneficiaries: "My dear "brother, JOHN LAWRANCE, does not stand in need "of any share of my property; but in token of my af- "fection for him, I do request his acceptance of and do "hereby bequeath to him my gold watch with its appur- "tenances." He gave to his wife, the whole of his household and kitchen furniture, as her own absolute property, of which no valuation was to be made, and one half of his entire estate. The remaining half, in trust, as to the interest or income of one-third part of such residue to be applied and appropriated to the use of the family of his brother Samuel, and the interest and income of the other two-third parts of such rest and residue to the sole use of his wife during her life, and after her decease, then the said two-thirds parts of the said rest and residue to the use of his said brother Samuel during his natural life, if he shall survive said wife; but, otherwise then the said rest and residue to be divided equally among the legal representatives of his said brother Samuel.

SAMUEL LAWRANCE, son of **Thomas** and **Ann** (Palmer) **Lawrance,** m. **HANNAH,** daughter of **John** and **Mary** (Norton) **Shinn,** of Springfield, Burlington County, New Jersey.

[John Shinn, (*Third*,) b. Nov. 25th, 1757, was a great-grand son of John Shinn, (*First*,) who landed at Burlington about 1680, and was one of the proprietors of New Jersey. His will is on record at Trenton, New Jersey, dated Jan. 14th, 1711. Jacob Shinn, grand-son of John, the proprietor, and father of John, first named, left the largest estate that had ever been settled in Burlington County. His will is dated January 10th, 1792, on record at Trenton. They were called, "the silk stocking family of Burlington County." John Shinn, first named, married Mary Norton, daughter of William and Susanna Norton, of Burlington County, New Jersey, and died 13th of February, 1833. They had two sons, who were respectably conspicuous in the society which they adorned: **WILLIAM NORTON SHINN** b. 24th Oct., 1782, m. **SALLY BUDD.** He died in August, 1871. He was elected Sheriff of Burlington County in 1825; to the State Council in 1829; re-elected in 1830, and again in 1831; to Congress in 1832, and re-elected in 1834; a vacancy occurring upon the Bench of the Court of Errors and Appeals, during the administration of his kinsman, Governor Fort, the latter, without the knowledge of Mr. Shinn, nominated him for the position; but the Senate failed to confirm the nomination; he was the *first* Director of the Camden and Amboy R. R. Co., on behalf of the State; a Director

of the Mount Holly Insurance Company; the Presiden
of the Burlington County Bible Society; and for half a
century, a most liberal and influential member of the
Board of Trustees of the Mount Holly Church.   JOHN
SHINN, Jr. (*Fourth,*) b. 19th Aug. 1784, m. MARY, daughter
of Dr. JOHN WHITE, of Philadelphia.   He was proposed for membership in "The First Troop Philadelphia City
Cavalry," by Robert Wharton, Esquire, Captain of the
Troop, and Mayor of the City of Philadelphia, and was
elected a member on 1st of Feb., 1806; he was an active member of the Troop until 26th August, 1814, when
he became "Honorary."   In 1811, he was Major 156th
Pa. Vol., and in 1814, Col. of 79th Pa. Vol., and in
1812 he was one of the *seven* founders of the Academy
of Natural Sciences, of Philadelphia, the other six being
Jacob Gilliams, M. D., C. M. Mann, N. S. Parmentier,
John Speakman, Thomas Say and Gerard Troost, M. D.
JOHN SHINN, Jr. died 16th October, 1825.]

SAMUEL and **HANNAH** (Shinn) **LAWRANCE**
had seven children: JOHN b. Oct. 16th, 1808. ANN b.
July 29th, 1810. THOMAS b. Feb. 1st, 1813. WILLIAM
SHINN b. Jan. 19th, 1815. MARY SHINN b. Dec. 26th,
1819. ELIZA GARDINER b. Feb. 24th, 1822, and ED-
WARD SHINN b. May 17th, 1825.   All deceased except ANN and EDWARD.

EDWARD SHINN LAWRANCE is now the
head of the **LAWRANCE** family of Philadelphia, although he is the youngest son of **Samuel,** who was
the youngest son of **Thomas,** of Philadelphia, who
died 1 mo. 30th, 1802, at No. 19 North Water Street,
Philadelphia, where he had lived many years, next door
South of the residence of Stephen Girard, who was then
looming up as Philadelphia's greatest merchant.   The
first Directory published in Philadelphia was for the
year of 1785.   It located Thomas Lawrance in Church
Alley, between Second and Third Streets.   The next

Yours very Respectfully —
Edward Shinn Lawrence

Directory published was for the year of 1791; it located him at No. 19 North Water Street, where he remained until his death, in 1802. In 1797 Stephen Girard moved into his house, next door to Thomas Lawrance, and continued to live there till his death, in 1831. The two houses were divided by Say's Alley, running to the river. The grounds extended to the river on each side of the Alley, as Delaware Avenue had not been opened. Stephen Girard was on the north side of the Alley, and Thomas Lawrance was on the south side of the Alley, and so they lived, next door neighbors, from 1797 to 1802. Every thing relating to Stephen Girard is interesting to Philadelphians. One cold, frosty morning, in winter, two children were playing with snow on Thomas Lawrance's porch towards the river. One was "Sam," the youngest son of Thomas Lawrance, and the other was Martha, a daughter of Richard Lawrance; they were cousins. Mr. Girard's habit was to go into his yard every morning, before breakfast, to wash his hands and face at his hydrant. He was washing as usual when "Sam" spied him across the alley, and full of childish glee and mischief, he said to Martha, "Oh! cousin Patty, there's old Steve; I'm going to snow-ball him." "Oh! no, cousin Sam, don't you do it." "Yes, I will, cousin Patty, and I'll make it hard, too," and he pressed the snow-ball in his hands between his knees and then threw it directly across the alley at Mr. Girard. At that moment Mr. Girard had finished washing and raised his head from the hydrant, his hands and face still wet, and was about to use his towel when the snow-ball hit him on the side of his head. The children were scared and scampered into the house. Mr. Girard, more surprised than hurt, cried out, "Oh! who is that trying to put my other eye out?" He had lost the sight of one of his eyes; he, however, opened the remaining one quickly enough to see "Sam" and call out to him, "Oh! you young rascal, I see you; I'll tell your father of you."

In a few moments Mr. Girard was knocking at neighbor Lawrance's front door; he complained of the unneighborly conduct of "Sam," who was properly punished for the offense, to Mr. Girard's satisfaction, according to the discipline of Friends.

"Sam" was Samuel Lawrance, father of Edward S. Lawrance, Esq., of Philadelphia.

"Patty" afterward became the wife of Seth Smith, of Philadelphia. She having participated in the above little incidents, related them with an enjoyable zest fifty years after they happened.

SAMUEL LAWRANCE was a minor when his father died in 1802. On 21st May, 1802, he petitioned the Orphan's Court, setting forth that his father, Thomas Lawrance, died some time since, leaving an estate, to a part of which he was entitled, that he was above the age of fourteen years and under the age of twenty-one years, and prayed that he might be permitted to choose a guardian to take charge of his person and estate during his minority. He made choice of Joseph Budd, and he was appointed.

THOMAS LAWRANCE'S will is on record at Philadelphia, dated 27th of 1st mo., 1802. Proved Feb. 5th, 1802. Executors: "Son **JOHN LAWRANCE** and esteemed Friend Elliston Perot." The estate was large. Beneficiaries: His nieces, Elizabeth Pearce, widow, Hannah Lawrance, Martha Lawrance, Susanna Lawrance, Sarah Lawrance, daughters of his brother Richard; his nephews Richard Lawrance, Jr. and Josiah Lawrance, sons of his brother Richard, each a legacy; his sister Mary Lawrance, a legacy; all the rest and residue of his estate to his three sons, John, Thomas, Jr., and Samuel, equally share and share alike. His son Thomas to have his household goods and kitchen furniture, his stock in trade, his horse and chaise and the harness thereto belonging, all to be appraised. "And provided lastly that notwith-

"standing anything herein before contained, my son Samuel
"shall be maintained, supported, educated, clothed and
"brought up at the cost and charge of my estate gener-
"ally until he shall attain the age of twenty-one years."

[THOMAS LAWRANCE, Jr., succeeded his
father at No. 19 North Water Street; the city Directories
locate him there and at Say's Wharf until 1810, when
he removed to No. 250 North Second Street, where he
remained till his death in 1811.]

EDWARD SHINN LAWRANCE, son of Sam-
uel and Hannah (Shinn) Lawrance, m. Nov. 20th,
1850, ARAMINTHA MARGARET ANNIE, daughter
of James Peyton and Aramintha (Hunter) Stuart.
[James Peyton Stuart was born in Virginia, in
1780, and died in Monongahela City, Pennsylvania, 17th
August, 1861. He was descended from some of the oldest and best families in "The Old Dominion." Before
he was of full age, he left his father's home and became *self-reliant*, that virtue of all virtues in Anglo-
American energy. He went direct to Old Red Stone
Fort, on the Monongahela River, and in a short time
was engaged in the flour trade down the Rivers Monongahela, Ohio and Mississippi, to New Orleans, when
Louisiana was a Spanish Province. Many years before
a steamboat was seen on the rivers, and when very few
of the human family other than savage American Indians
could be seen on their banks, he would load his "Flat-
boats" with barrels of flour at "old-red-stone-fort," and
let them float with the current down to New Orleans,
where he would sell the flour and the boats, and return
by sea to Philadelphia or New York and thence to "Old
Red Stone Fort" for a new venture. After a few years,
having accumulated considerable property, and Pittsburg,
being still a Borough, he settled his family there and
embarked largely in the dry goods trade; for nearly a
quarter of a century he was the leading dry goods mer-

chant in Pittsburg. After the great fire, which consumed Pittsburg in 1845, he retired from business and spent the remainder of his life on the banks of the Monongahela River, whose bosom had yielded him his first gains, in the enjoyment of an ample fortune, honestly acquired, and the respect of all who knew him, as a man of wonderful energy and unimpeachable integrity.]

EDWARD SHINN and ARAMINTHA M. A. (Stuart) LAWRANCE have children:

JAMES PEYTON STUART b. Aug. 6th, 1852, a graduate of "The Lehigh University," Class of '73, in the School of Mechanical Engineering; Degree, M. E. On 22d March, 1875, commissioned an Assistant Engineer in the U. S. Navy. He wears the gold medal of the University, for the best Essay, of his class, in English. The subject being "The Lehigh Valley."

EDWARD STUART b. Jany. 25th, 1854; a matriculate of "The Lehigh University," spent his Freshman and Sophomore years there, left in June, 1873, studied surgery and medicine with the distinguished Surgeon, Dr. F. F. Maury, of Philadelphia; graduated, taking the degree of M. D. at "The Jefferson Medical College of Philadelphia," in March, 1879, his subject of Thesis being "Delirium Tremens." He is a member of "The First Troop Philadelphia City Cavalry," elected 5th Jan'y, 1874. He was elected a member of "The Philadelphia County Medical Society," on Oct. 20th, 1880, and, same year, elected an Assistant on the Surgical Clinic of The Jefferson Medical College Hospital.

JOSIAH RANDALL b. Sept. 17th, 1856, a matriculate of "The Jefferson Medical College of Philadelphia."

WILLIAM HUNTER b. Oct. 26th, 1858, a Cadet Engineer, second class, U. S. Naval Academy, Annapolis, Maryland, appointed October 1st, 1879.

ST. LAWRENCE JACKSON b. March 19th, 1862, a matriculate of "The University of Pennsylvania," Towne Scientific School.

EDWARD STUART LAWRANCE, M. D., m.
21st July, 1879, his first cousin, JEANIE LETITIA, only child of Andrew Jackson and Margaret Ann (Sampson) Stuart. They have a son JACKSON STUART, b. 5th June, 1880.

[From **RICHARD** of London, to **JACKSON STU-ART**, of Philadelphia, born in 1880, both inclusive, seven generations of males, in a direct line.]

EDWARD S. LAWRANCE, Esq., of Philadelphia, read Law with Josiah Randall. Esq., of Philadelphia; during his minority his uncle, the honorable **WILLIAM NORTON SHINN**, of Burlington County, New Jersey, was the guardian of his person and estate; on June 2d, 1847, on Mr. Randall's motion, he was admitted to practice in the courts of Philadelphia, and on 10th December, 1849, on motion of Mr. Randall. he was admitted to practice in The Supreme Court of Pennsylvania.

In 1853, The Select and Common Councils of Philadelphia, elected him a School Director, to fill the unexpired term of Francis Wharton, Esq., resigned.

In 1854, he was elected again by the Councils, and after the consolidation of the city in that year, he was elected to the same office by the people, for one year.

In 1855, he was elected again to the same office by the people, for a term of three years, which he resigned in October of that year.

In 1858, he was a Corporator and Treasurer of The Philadelphia College of Medicine.

On the 7th of January, 1864, he was elected a member of "The First Troop Philadelphia City Cavalry," and continued active until March 6th, 1876, when his name was transferred, upon his own application, to the non-active roll of the Company.

[The First Centennial Anniversary of The Troop was 17th November, 1874. It was celebrated for three days, November 15th, 16th and 17th, in a grand and imposing manner. A beautiful and costly badge, composed of silver and gold, was conferred on each and every member who turned out with The Troop, in uniform, on those three days, to be held in perpetuity by himself and his family, in commemoration of the event. **Mr. LAW-RANCE** and his son, **EDWARD STUART LAWRANCE,** **M. D.,** have two of those badges, as both, father and son, turned out together as active members in uniform. A similar circumstance could not be recalled in the history of The Troop.]

He was a Corporation Trustee and Chairman of the Board of Corporation Trustees of "The Hahnemann Medical College of Philadelphia;" *also*, a Manager and a Trustee and Chairman of the Board of Trustees of The Hospital of "The Hahnemann Medical College of Philadelphia," from 1867 until his resignation in 1878.

He was one of the *founders*, and the First Warden and a Vestryman of "The Church of The Good Shepherd," Radnor, Pennsylvania.

His most conspicuous professional labor was his conduct of the settlement of the affairs of The Honorable John Nicholson, of Philadelphia, who was the first Controller General of Pennsylvania, and who was connected with The Honorable Robert Morris, of revolutionary renown, and James Greenleaf, Esq., in the latter part of the last century, in very extended landed speculations. they had issued their negotiable paper for over two mil: lions of dollars, which caused them to fail financially in 1798; they were all incarcerated in the Philadelphia Prison, in which Mr. Nicholson died in 1800. They had established "The North American Land Company" in 1795, with six millions of acres of land—*also*, a Trust, to secure their notes amounting to $2,000,000; *also*, "The Aggregate Fund" Deed, which contained a large part of the land on which now stands the City of Washington, and several other land companies. These very important matters have had Mr. Lawrance's attention for a period of twenty-five years and they are still unsettled; the cases have gone from court to court and three times to The Supreme Court of Pennsylvania—See 7 Wright: 10 P. F.

Smith: and 2 Norris. They have claimed the attention of the best legal ability in Philadelphia. Mr. Lawrance is now the administrator of the estate of John Nicholson, deceased, having been appointed on the 20th of March, 1874. His offices are at No. 206 West Washington Square, where they have been continuously since 1st August, 1857.

Mr. LAWRANCE'S *four* great-grand fathers bore the surnames of **Lawrance, Shinn, Norton,** and **Palmer.** Three of them, **Lawrance, Norton,** and **Palmer,** have been ennobled and emblazoned in Heraldry, in England. The remaining one, **Shinn,** seems not to have been so prominent a name in England; but when New Jersey was planted, that name took deep root in her virgin soil. No family in New Jersey have for the same time, covering a period of two hundred years, been more respected, or held more wealth, power and influence, in New Jersey, than the family which sprang from the loins of **John Shinn,** *the proprietor.*

The **LAWRENCES** and the **WASHINGTONS,** in England, quartered their arms, and in America a **LAURENS** precedes the **WASHINGTON** in the Presidency of the country. **HENRY LAURENS** was our first President.

4.   **JOSIAH LAWRANCE,** son of **Thomas** and **Susanna** (Van Eman) **Lawrance,** died 7th of 9th mo., 1774, unmarried.

5.   **JESSE LAWRANCE,** son of **Thomas** and **Susanna** (Van Eman) **Lawrance,** died 27th of 9th mo., 1749, in infancy.

6.   **RICHARD LAWRANCE,** son of **Thomas** and **Susanna** (Van Eman) **Lawrance,** married **REBEKAH LEWIS,** daughter of **Jacob Lewis, Esq.,** of Philadelphia. His town residence was on the South side of Walnut Street, East of Third Street; the grounds

ran southward to St. Paul's Church. They had one child only: JACOB LEWIS b. 2d of 4th mo., 1774, d. 5th of 1st mo., 1775. The mother died soon afterward.

RICHARD LAWRANCE married again to **MARY**, daughter of **John** and **Hannah Milnor**.

They had children:

MILNOR b. 11th mo. 5th, 1776, d. 7th mo. 26th, 1777.

ELIZABETH b. 9th mo. 25th, 1779, m. GEORGE PRYOR, d. 8th mo. 16th, 1813.

HANNAH b. 7th mo., 22d, 1783, d. 28th of 6th mo., 1809; m. JOHN CORNEAU.

RICHARD b. 2d mo. 12th, 1785, d. 12th mo., 27th, 1814, unmarried.

MARTHA b. 11th mo. 15th, 1787, m. SETH SMITH.

DAVID b. 7th mo. 4th, 1789, d. 7th mo. 27th, 1790.

SUSANNA b. 11th mo. 24th, 1790, d. 7th mo. 1st, 1791.

JOSIAH b. 6th mo. 5th, 1792. See presently.

SARAH b. 7th mo. 21tt, 1794.

SUSANNA (2d) b. 9th mo. 10th, 1795, m. ISRAEL LEEDS.

LETISAH.

JOSIAH, son of Richard and Mary (Milnor) Lawrance, m. **MARTHA ANN**, b. April 7th, 1793, daughter of **Thomas Davis** and **Abigail Cook Conover**. Josiah d. in 1851, and Martha Ann, his widow, Sept. 6th, 1878. They had children: 1. Charles Conover died when about five years of age. 2. Caroline E. deceased. 3. RICHARD CHARLES b. Sept. 12th, 1816, m. March 4th, 1844, LUCY JANE b. March 17th, 1824, daughter of Captain Andrew and Lucy Woodbury Marsters, of Manchester by the Sea. 4. John Gardiner d. unmarried.

RICHARD CHARLES and **LUCY JANE** (Marsters) **LAWRANCE** had children: 1. RICHARD CHARLES, Jr. b. March 28th, 1846, in Charlestown, Massachu-

GENEALOGICAL NOTES.

setts, m. **JULIA A. BASFORD**, of Chester, New Hampshire. In the late war, he enlisted in the 18th New Hampshire Regiment, and at the close of the war was with his Regiment doing guard duty, in Washington, over the prisoners implicated in the murder of President Lincoln. He was commissioned Captain of Company G, of the 8th Regiment, by Governor Talbot. 2. **MARIA LOUISE** b. April 4th, 1850, d. Sept. 16th, 1851. 3. **LUCY** b. Oct. 1st, 1855. 4. **MARY MILNOR** b. Feb. 9th, 1860. 5. **ANDREW MARSTERS** b. April 5th, 1864, d. Sept. 11th, 1865.

RICHARD CHARLES LAWRANCE, Jr., [son of Richard Charles and Lucy Jane (Marsters) Lawrance,] and **JULIA A. (Basford) LAWRANCE**, have had children: 1. **MABEL J.** 2. **EDWARD** d. when 3 years old. 3. **GUY.**

From **RICHARD**, of London, to **GUY**, both inclusive, seven generations of males in a direct line.

RICHARD CHARLES LAWRANCE, Esquire, of Gloucester, Massachusetts, is now the head of the only branch of the family, bearing the name, in this country, other than that branch of Philadelphia, of which **EDWARD SHINN LAWRANCE, Esquire,** is now the head.

7. **JASON LAWRANCE**, son of Thomas and Susanna (Van Eman) Lawrance, married **MARY O'BRIEN**, a beautiful Creole, of New Orleans. Louisiana being then a Province of Spain. So exuberant and luxuriant was her hair, that when let loose, it would reach down to her feet, and she would envelop her entire body in it. She was familiarly called "La belle Sauvage."

She bore him one son only: **JASON O'BRIEN.**

JASON, her husband, died about 1796, leaving her a widow. She afterward married **Dr. FLOOD**, of New Orleans.

57

JASON O'BRIEN, son of Jason and Mary (O'Brien) Lawrance, was born in New Orleans, in 1791, and was a minor when his father died. After his uncle David Lawrance died, in Philadelphia, he petitioned the Justices of the Orphans' Court for permission to choose a guardian, stating that by the death of his uncle David Lawrance he was entitled to certain personal estate in the City of Philadelphia, that his father was dead and his mother lived in New Orleans; he named his cousin Thomas Lawrance and he was appointed. In 1808, Thomas Lawrance renounced the office, and Chandler Price, a prominent merchant, was appointed in his place. He graduated at "The University of Pennsylvania," taking the degree of M. D. in 1815, having been six years engaged in study at the time when he received his diploma. His residence was Louisiana, and his "subject of essay" was "Fractures of the Thigh Bone." He returned to New Orleans and began the practice of medicine with his stepfather Dr. FLOOD. In 1818 Dr. LAWRANCE came back to Philadelphia. He had ambition and capacity to be a teacher; but not considering it expedient to set up in opposition to the University, he believed that there was opportunity for a successful season for private practice between the time when the University lectures closed in March, and the resumption in November. Acting upon that theory, he *founded* the Philadelphia School of Anatomy in March, 1820. He lectured six times a week, "and his personal qualities, as well as his ease and perspicuity as a lecturer, made his school a decided success." In the fall of 1820, he was made assistant to Dr. Gibson, Professor of Surgery at the University, and in 1822 also an assistant to Dr. Horner, then Adjunct Professor of Anatomy. These positions did not interfere with the anatomical school, which was a summer arrangement. In the summer of 1822, he, assisted by Drs. Harlan and Coates, members of a committee appointed by the Academy of Medicine, made upwards of ninety experiments on living animals, in order to determine the correctness of the theory of Magendie that absorption was posssible by other channels than by the absorbent vessels, especially by the veins. In 1823 he and Dr. Coates performed over one hundred experiments upon living animals for the same purpose. They also commenced experiments to determine absorption by the brain; before they were concluded Dr. LAWRANCE died on the 19th of August, 1823, at No. 139 South Fifth Street, Philadelphia, from the effects of typhoid fever, which he caught while attending the poor in the Ridge road district. He was surgeon to the Philadelphia Hospital. Had life been spared him, he would undoubtedly have become a great teacher. He was a perfect enthusiast, and cared nothing for personal danger. In New Orleans he had performed autopsies on the bodies of victims of yellow fever, which were pronounced reckless in their character. In 1820 he left a complete record of such examinations. It is probable that he was one of the first persons in Philadelphia to practice vivisection. He was an officer of The Phrenological Society and a member of The American Philosophical Society. In 1814–15, he was a resident Physician in the Pennsylvania Hospital. He married MARY ROBISON MIFFLIN, the only sister of the late Benjamin Mifflin. They had one child only: MARY F., who died unmarried. Dr. LAWRANCE died intestate. Dr. Coates wrote an Obituary Notice of him, and Professor Samuel Jackson wrote his Eulogium; both are published at length, in the Philadelphia Jour. Med. and Phys. Sci. 1823, at pages 171 and 376. His estate went to his widow and only child, MARY F. The child being about two years of age, her mother was appointed her guardian. After her mother's death, Stephen Baldwin and Henry A. Boardman were, in March, 1835, appointed her guardians, she being under fourteen years of age; in August, 1836, she being then over fourteen years of age, her Uncle Benjamin Mifflin was appointed her guardian, on her petition, and Stephen

Baldwin and Henry A. Boardman were agreeably to their request discharged by the Court. She died in her minority, intestate, and her Uncle Benjamin Mifflin became her administrator; an auditor, appointed by the Court, divided her estate among her uncles: Benjamin Mifflin, Henry Mifflin, Edward Mifflin and Thomas Mifflin, and Henry Flood, a half brother, and Catherine Flood, a half sister of her father; in equal shares. No LAWRANCE appeared to make a claim to any part of it.

8.   ISAAC LAWRANCE, son of Thomas and Susanna (Van Eman) Lawrance, died 10th mo. 23d, 1753, in infancy, not one month old.

9.   SAMUEL LAWRANCE, son of Thomas and Susanna (Van Eman) Lawrance, d. 11th mo. 11th day, 1817; testate and unmarried. His will is recorded at Mount Holly, New Jersey; dated 8th day of 10th mo., 1817. He gave his entire estate to his brother Richard and sister Mary, and named his brother Richard as sole executor.

10.   MARY LAWRANCE, daughter of Thomas and Susanna (Van Eman) Lawrance, d. 2d mo. 24th, 1837; testate and unmarried. Her will is recorded at Mount Holly, New Jersey; dated 22d of 11th mo., 1836; proved March 8th, 1837. Peter De Cou, Executor. Beneficiaries: Her nieces, Amy Fenimore, Susanna Folwell, Susanna Leeds, Martha Smith (wife of Seth); grandnieces, Elizabeth Folwell, Ann Folwell, Susanna Folwell, Esther G. Fenimore, Elizabeth G. Lawrance, Caroline E. Lawrance, Mary Leeds, Margaret Leeds; grandnephews, John Folwell, Richard Lawrance, Samuel L. Smith (son of Seth). _____

The two brothers, Thomas and Richard, had precisely the same domestic experience in early life:

Thomas married first Hannah Hallowell, who bore him a son, named John, after his grandfather John

Hallowell. The child and his mother both died young, and **Thomas** married secondly **Ann Palmer,** by whom he had his family.

Richard married first Rebekah Lewis, who bore him a son, named Jacob Lewis, after his grandfather Jacob Lewis. The child and his mother both died young, and **Richard** married secondly **Mary Milnor,** by whom he had his family.

A remarkable coincidence.

DAVID LAWRANCE, when he was about fifty years of age, went over to London, to look after some property interest for the family. He landed at Bristol, the 7th mo. 9th, 1789, and remained in England until about 1796. He took his father's family Bible with him.

Soon after his arrival in London, he found it would be necessary to file a Bill in Chancery. A Bill was drawn, dated 26th November, 1789, and filed: "David Lawrance and others against Samuel Dixon and others," which was pending six or seven years.

The contention was for a sum of £2000 sterling. The final termination of the suit was as follows:

"*Upon* opening debate in the matter and hearing "the same, order dated the 20th day of July, 1791, the "said decree dated the 5th day of February, 1793, the "said Masters report dated the 22d day of June, 1795, "a letter of attorney signed Thomas Lawrance, Richard "Lawrance, Samuel Lawrance and Mary Lawrance, dated "the 5th day of June, 1789, an order dated the 3d day "of July, 1795, a decree of attorney signed Jason Law-"rance and the account of general certificate read and "what was alleged by the Court on both sides. His "Honor doth order that the cash in bank standing in "the name of the Accountant General of this Court on "the credit of this cause be paid the plaintiff David "Lawrance—one-sixth part thereof in his own right and

"the remaining five-sixth parts thereof in trust for the
"five persons, Thomas Lawrance, Richard Lawrance Jason
"Lawrance, Samuel Lawrance and Mary Lawrance, his
"brothers and sister, in equal shares. *And it is* further
"*ordered* that the papers and writings deposited with the
"said Master belonging to the plaintiff be delivered to the
"plaintiff as belonging to him in his own right, and in
"trust for the benefit of the said other persons, and that
"the papers and writings deposited with the said master
"belonging to the defendant, be delivered to the defend-
"ant who deposited the same, and for the purpose as-
"signed, the said Accountant General is to draw on the
"bank, according to the form prescribed by the Act of
"Parliament, and the General Rule and Orders of the Court
"in that case made and provided.

"P. W."

The following letters relate to the same subject matter:

"LONDON, 2d mo. 5, 1793.

"Esteemed Friend,
            "I was in hopes of seeing thee during
"my stay here; and some days ago hearing thou had
"called at the Poultry but an hour or two before I got
"there from Walthamstow; I staid within in the expec-
"tation of thy calling again. I much wish to know the
"present situation of thy suit, and thy prospect of end-
"ing it. A line of information left or addressed to No.
"10 Poultry will reach me at Brighton, and be very ac-
"ceptable. I am about returning to my family, after an
"absence of near three weeks. They were in pretty good
"health, and likely to continue there some months. If I
"can in anywise serve thee, I wish thee to mention wherein
"with freedom.

"With respects to our friend Borrett,
      "I am thy sincere friend,

"Wm. Dillwyn.

"The old proverb says: "New brooms sweep clean."
"I hope the present Chancellor, at least on setting out,

"will be more inclined to *Dispatch*, than his predecessor:
"and that at least *one* Chancery suit may end in the
"reign in which it commenced."

THOMAS BORRETT, Esq.

SHOREHAM, near

SEVEN OAKS,

For   KENT.

DAVID LAWRANCE.

PHILADELPHIA, 12th mo. 20th, 1794.

Dear Brother:
I received thy letter per the *Tiger*, dated
the 9th mo., and am sorry to find thee has been obliged
to have recourse to the law again for a settlement of that
troublesome business; it is a most surprising thing, as
our proofs have been made to satisfaction, that there
should be such an astonishing delay in their giving a
decree. Is there no such thing as having an interview
with the Lord Chancellor, and representing the case to
him? I understand Jno. Elmsley did in Hallowell's case.
It has been upward of five years since thee went over and a
considerable time since the proofs have been made in our fa-
vor; there seems but little for them to do in the case but
to allow Dixon what they think Aunt had of Wright's
estate. His conduct from the beginning has been very
wide from what I should expect from an honest man: in
the first place he never, that we were informed of, sent
over to make any enquiry for our father, in order to re-
mit him the £1,000 legacy, and when thee went over he
would give thee no opportunity of an interview with him
for years, and I believe his last proposal was for no other end
than to spin out time. Thee has not informed me if he has
given security, perhaps he may make away all his property, he has so many years for it. I am afraid our Attorney is deficient in his duty. There is a friend, Nicholas Waln, recommended thee to Joseph Gurney Bevan, a
very capable man. I find his name as Clerk to the yearly
Meeting of London's Epistle; I think it would be well to

advise with him on the case, as it is likely to take its course in law, thro' his base conduct. I hope thee will come upon no other terms with him than what he is allowed by the Court, and, as for Court charges, I think it very unjust if a dishonest man gets possession of his neighbor's property and stands a suit with him for years and is cast, he shall be at no expense, but his neighbor's property must pay all. I am informed there is an action open against him for charges. I am very sorry for our relation Borrett's misconduct, and hope his misfortune may have a tendency to reclaim him. I have desired Brother Samuel to write no more there; he informed me he did not know they had postage to pay, but he did not say he would or would not write again. If thee should be favored to get any part of the property more than the expenses, I think best of lodging it in William Dillwyn's hands, till we should draw for it. Exchange is very high here now, upward of eighty. We are, thanks to the Lord, in as good health as common; hoping these may find thee better than when thee wrote. William Lovet Smith was buried last fourth-day, he died with the colic. We are favored here with peace and a mild Government, while most part of Europe is convulsed with war and devastation; for which I hope we may be truly thankful. So conclude with hopes we may be favored to see thee in the Spring, and remain thy loving brother,

THOMAS LAWRANCE.

WILLIAM DILLWYN,
No. 10 POULTRY,
For   LONDON.
DAVID LAWRANCE.
per Brig *Holbrook*.

The next page following, is the title page of the family Bible of **THOMAS LAWRANCE,** born in London, A. D. 1707. It was sent to him from London, *by his cousin*, THOMAS LAWRANCE, A. D. 1750.

THE HOLY

BIBLE,

Containing the OLD and NEW

TESTAMENTS:

Newly Translated out of the ORIGINAL TONGUES:

AND WITH THE FORMER

TRANSLATIONS

DILIGENTLY

COMPARED AND REVISED.

By His Majesty's Special Command.

Appointed to be read in CHURCHES.

OXFORD:

Printed by THOMAS BASKETT. Printer to the UNIVERSITY.

MDCCXLVII.

A.

In Chancery.

This Book was shown to William Dillwyn on his Examination for David Lawrance and others Complts., agt. Samuel Dixon and others, Defendants.

HENRY FLITCROFT,

by H. B. Dep'y.

(a.)

Thomas Lawrance and Susannah Lawrance: Bible. Sent from London by their Couzen Thomas Lawrance, in the year 1750.

Thomas Lawrance, son of Richard and Margaret Lawrance, was born in London, Annq Domii 1707.

Sis Fidelis Usque ad Mortem et Dabo ubi 'coronam Vitæ —— Apocylap'' ————

(b.)

The Ages of Thomas and Susannah Lawrance's Children, viz:

David Lawrance was Born 7th mo. 21st, 1739.

Elizabeth Lawrance was Born 12th mo. 25th, Annq Domii 1740-1.

Thomas Lawrance was born 1 mo. 7th, 1742-3.

Josiah Lawrance was born 6 mo. 14th, 1745.

Jesse Lawrance was born 8 mo. 7th, 1747, and departed this life the 9th month 27th, 1749.

Richard Lawrance was born 8 mo. 16th, 1749.

Jason Lawrance was Born ye 5th mo. 3d, 1751, afternoon.

Isaac Lawrance was Born 9 mo. 30th, Anno 1753 N. S., and departed this life ye 10th mo. 23 . . . 53 N. S.

Samuel Lawrance was Born, viz: the 2d day of 11 month, at Night, Annq Domii 1755 N. S.

Mary Lawrance was Born, viz: the 5th mo. 16th, @ break of Day, Anno Domii 1758 N. S.

(c.)

Thomas Lawrance, Son of Richard Lawrance and Margaret Lawrance, was Born in London Annq Domii 1707.

Susannah Lawrance, Daughter of David Van Eman and Eleanor Van Eman and Espoused wife of the above Thomas Lawrance, was Born Annq Domii 1718.

David Lawrance, Son of the above named Thomas and Susannah Lawrance, was Born 7 month 21st, Annq Domii 1739.

Elizabeth Lawrance was Born 12 month 25th, Annq Domii 1741.

Thomas Lawrance was Born, viz: 1st month 7th, Annq Domii 1743.

Josiah Lawrance was Born, viz: 6th month 14th, Annq Domii 1745.

Jesse Lawrance was Born, viz: 8th month 7th, Annq Domii 1747, departed this life 9 month 27th, Annq Domii 1749.

Richard Lawrance was Born, viz: 8 month 16th, Annq Domii 1749.

Jason Lawrance was Born, viz: 5th month 3d, Annq Domii 1751.

Isaac Lawrance was born, viz: the 9th month 30th, Annq Domii 1753 N. S., and departed this life ye 10th mo. 23d, '53.

Samuel Lawrance was Born, viz: 11th month 2d day, at night, Annq Domii 1755.

Mary Lawrance was born 5th mo. 16th, Anno Do 1758.

(d.)

Mary Lawrance was Born, viz: 5th month 16th @ break of Day, Anno 1758 N. S.

So the family record appeared in the Bible when the Bible was put in evidence, in the suit in Chancery.

The large "A," and the small (a.) (b.) (c.) and (d.), were so marked by the Master in Chancery, that he could refer to them as Exhibits, in making his Report.

THE BIBLE was brought home again by **DAVID LAWRANCE,** and passed into the possession of his sister **MARY,** who bequeathed it to her niece **AMY FENIMORE,** and after her death it went into the possession of her daughter **Hetty,** who, with great liberality, presented it to **EDWARD S. LAWRANCE,** as the head of the **Lawrance family** of Philadelphia. It has been read and highly valued by five generations.

Mr. LAWRANCE, of Philadelphia, has in his possession another book, printed in LONDON, 1740, which belonged to his great-grandfather, **Thomas Lawrance,** entitled "The Young Mathematician's Guide: Being a Plain and Easy Introduction to the MATHEMATICKS." In Five Parts. By JOHN WARD. Dedicated To the *Honorable Sir* RICHARD GROSVENOR, of *Eaton,* in the County *Palatine* of Chester, BARONET.

On its inner cover is the following inscription:—

‘‘*Thomæ*’’ ‘‘*Laurentius.*)
Thomas Lawrance’’ . . .
*Est Verus Pofsefsor–Hujus, Libri,
Londinenfis*’’.*Annq' Domii.* 1751.
Ætatis' Suæ. 45.

At that time Books were very scarce in the Province of New Jersey.

JOSIAH RANDALL LAWRANCE, *third child* of **Edward Shinn** and **Aramintha Margaret Annie** (Stuart) **Lawrance,** studied medicine with his Brother **Dr. Edward Stuart Lawrance,** and graduated at The Jefferson Medical College of Philadelphia, on the 30th of March, 1882, taking the Degree of M. D. His subject of Thesis was, "Pathology of Typhoid Fever."

[RICHARD CHARLES LAWRANCE, Jr., enlisted July 25th, 1864, in the Martin Guards, a New Hampshire Company, for coast defence, and was discharged Sept. 16th, 1864. He enlisted again Jan'y 26th, 1865, in Company H, 18th Reg't New Hampshire Volunteers, and served till July 28th, 1865. This Reg't was attached to the 9th Army Corps before Petersburg. A the engagement at Fort Stedman he was promoted Corporal. In 1871, he was Sergeant of Company G., 8th Reg't Infantry, Massachusetts Volunteer Militia; May 23d, 1873, promoted to Second Lieutenant, and Nov. 18th, 1874, to Captain: commissioned by Gov. Talbot, of Massachussetts. On July 29th, 1878, discharged at his own request. This Regiment received a complimentary letter of thanks from Congress. It was sent by the Governor of Massachusetts, to Philadelphia, in 1876, and is considered the best Reg't in Massachusetts.]

EDWARD SHINN LAWRANCE, second child of Dr. Edward Stuart and Jeanie Letitia (Stuart Lawrance, was born on the second of April, 1882.

He is EDWARD S. LAWRANCE, 3d, and from RICHARD LAWRANCE, of London, both inclusive, the seventh generation of males in a direct line.

LAWRENCE!—MEN, gallant in chivalry—brave in battle on land and sea—learned in art, science, law, medicine and theology—canonized in the Church for courage, charity and piety—wise in magistracy, diplomacy and Senates—successful in commerce and finance—you have given to England an Archbishop of Canterbury; a Premier; a Viceroy of India; one of her most eminent

Painters; a President of the Royal Academy; and to her Capital, Aldermen, Sheriffs and Lord Mayors. In return you have received great honors and decorations. It would be tedious to enumerate and describe the many Coats of Arms conferred upon you. Your lineage is one of the proudest in the land.

"The Lawrences were allied to all that was great and "illustrious; cousins to the ambitious Dudley, Duke of "Northumberland; to the Earl of Warwick; to Lord "Guilford Dudley, who expiated on the scaffold the "short-lived royalty of Lady Jane Gray; to the brilliant "Leicester, who set two queens at variance; and to Sir "Philip, Sidney, who refused a throne."

> "LAWRENCE!—the name to future years shall live,
> "Shall greatly live, till time's memorial dies;
> "Merit to merit shall its tribute give,
> "And Italy's proud sons yield up the prize."
>
> —"MELUSINA."

European Magazine, 1796, *Vol.* 29, *page* 275.

Thomas.

THOMAS.

PHILIP THOMAS, of the mercantile firm of Thomas and Devonshire, at Bristol, England, b. about 1600, is the earliest *proven* ancestor of this family. An old tradition connects the family with the first Norman Archbishop of York, Thomas de Douvre d. 1100, whose brother Sampson was Bishop of–Worcester, but it is totally without foundation. The coat of arms borne by the Emigrant ancestor (argent, a chevron checquy of or and' sable between three ravens close of the last) on his gold headed cane, and service of silver, leads me rather to connect him with the celebrated Sir Rhys ap Thomas K. G. of Carew Castle, Pembrokeshire, South Wales, who bore argent, a chevron sable, between three ravens close of the last. These arms were authenticated for Philip E. Thomas by the late Sir Charles G. Young Garter King at Arms. The connection with the Knight of Carew I formerly attempted to trace through a supposed younger son of his unfortunate grandson and heir Rice ap Griffith, by the name of Thomas, but the State paper relied on to sup- port this by mentioning him as with James ap Griffiith his father's cousin, at the Court of Scotland, does not do so, and I am at present unable to say whose son he was. I find him in the latter part of the sixteenth cen- tury occupying land in the parish of Ebbernant in Caer- marthenshire, Wales. He md. Sybell dau. of Philip Scidamore, and' his wife Joan, widow of Walter Kyrle ; and grandau. of John Scudamore, a Gentleman Usher to

73

K. Henry VIII. She brought him the demesne lands of Grosmant Manor, Monmouthshire, and a grist mill nĕar by. Their son John Philip Thomas inherited this before 1585, and in 1591 was Queen's lessee of mills at Kenchurch in the same Shire. I have supposed him to be the Emigrant's grandfather by Evan Thomas of Swansea b. 1580 d. 1650, whose name begins the Pedigree of the family compiled by the late Philip E. Thomas. As his papers upon the pedigree have been lost I cannot say what authority he had for the existence and citizenship of this Evan Thomas. I find notices of an Evan Thomas who was a member of the Awennydion or College of Bards of Glamorgan in 1620; and a Captain Evan Thomas who was one of the principal members of a Baptist Congregation, near Swansea, in 1672; but I do not know if either or both are the same with Evan of Swansea. Philip Thomas, the Emigrant, may have been the Philip Thomas in the the East India Company's service in 1621, and in London in 1638 as a Messenger of the Commissioners for Charitable Uses. He certainly emigrated to the Province of Maryland in 1651. The earliest record of a land grant to him dated February 19th, 1651–2, conveys to him 500 acres of land called "Beckley" on the west side of Chesapeake Bay "in consideration that he hath in the year 1651 transported himself, Sarah his wife, Philip, Sarah, and Elizabeth his children into this our province." Between 1658 and 1661 he had granted him 100 acres called "Thomas Towne," in 1665 a grant of 120 acres called "Fuller's Poynt," in 1668 a grant of 300 acres called "The Planes," in 1672 a grant of 200 acres called "Phillip's Addicion," and numerous other grants of unnamed tracts. This land lay mostly in Anne Arundel County and in the neighborhood of what is now known as West River. "Fuller's Poynt" between the Severn and South Rivers is now known as Thomas' Point, and in the site of a light-house. A man of character and position, he acquired considerable influence in the affairs of the Colony, and became one of the leaders of the Puritan party. When under Capt. William Fuller, the Puritans gained possession of the Government, he was appointed a member of the Provincial Council, and when in 1658 they were compelled to resign their control, he was one of the commissioners to make the surrender.

March 20th, 1658-9, says the old Council Record Book, Liber Hh. "Messrs. Wm. Fuller, Edward Lloyd, Richard Preston, Samuel Withers, Philip Thomas, and Thomas Mears came to St. Leonards in order to the performance of the Articles of Surrender of the Government as intended and arranged between Richard Bennet and others and the Lord Proprietary's Officers, November 30th, 1657.

After this he did not take an active part in the political affairs of the Colony, and seems to have joined the Society of Friends previous to his death. The celebrated George Fox visiting Maryland, Philip Thomas may have been converted to that persuasion by his preaching. His Will was made September 9th, 1674, and probated July 10th, 1675. After her husband's death SARAH THOMAS (according to Philip E. Thomas, "born Sarah Harrison") was a prominent member and probably a minister of the Society of Friends. She d. early in 1687 having had issue:

Born in England before 1651;

PHILIP d. s. p. before 1688; SARAH m. in 1674 JOHN, son of Thomas and Elizabeth Mears, who d. in May, 1675, and his wife the same year, leaving issue: SARAH; ELIZABETH m. as his 3d wife WILLIAM COALE, (q. v.) he d. Oct 30th, 1678, and she m. before 1683 EDWARD TALBOT (q. v.) and d. in 1726;

Born in Maryland:

MARTHA m. after 1672 RICHARD ARNELL or ARNOLD who d. in May 1683, she d. before 1688 having had issue:

SAMUEL d. i.; SARAH, and ELIZABETH b. Dec. 24th, 1682 m. 1st Jany. 8th, 1702 JACOB GILES and had issue Sarah, and 2d July 30th, 1704 THOMAS HAWKINS; SAMUEL, of whom presently:

SAMUEL, only surviving son of Philip and Sarah (Harrison) Thomas, b. about 1655, was probably a Minister of the Society of Friends as early as 1686, when he received a certificate to visit Philadelphia Yearly Meeting, from West River Monthly Meeting. He m. May 15th, 1688, at his own house in Anne Arundel County, MARY, youngest dau of Francis and Elizabeth Hutchins, of Calvert County, who d. in July 1751. He died before 1743, having had issue:

SARAH b. March 31st, 1689, m. Oct. 25th, 1705, JOSEPH RICHARDSON (q. v.); SAMUEL b. Feby. 1st, 1691, d. i.; SAMUEL, the 2nd, b. March 11th, 1693, d. i.; PHILIP b. March 1st, 1694, of whom presently; JOHN b. April 15th, 1697 (q. v); ELIZABETH b. Dec. 28th, 1698, m. Dec. 19th, 1717, RICHARD SNOWDEN, (q. v.); MARY b. Nov. 6th, 1700, m. July 31st, 1718, JOHN GALLOWAY (q. v.); SAMUEL, the 3d, b. Nov. 12th, 1702, (q. v.); ANN m. Oct. 8th, 1730, EDWARD FELL, of Over Kittel, Lancashire, Eng., who d. in March 1743, leaving issue: ANNE; and MARGARET b. 1710, m. after 1735, WILLIAM HARRIS (q. v.).

PHILIP, eldest son of Samuel and Mary Thomas, b. March 1st, 1694, md. 1st in March 1721, FRANCES HOLLAND, and had issue by her: WILLIAM, of whom presently. He married 2dly August 11th, 1724, ANN, dau. of Samuel and Mary Chew, and died November 23d, 1762, his wife May 22nd, 1777, having had issue:

ARMS OF CHEW.

SAMUEL b. June 12th, 1725, (q. v.): PHILIP b. July 3d, 1727, (q. v.); MARY b. Jany. 1st, 1730-1, md 1st, May 12th,

HENRIETTA MARGARET
, ho d. in July 1809, his
2dly, Feby. 7th, 1760,
· of Virginia, by whom she
—H b. March 8th, 1732–3,
RICHARD b. July 17th,
had issue: PHILIP md.
EPHEN STEWART, before
m, 1743 (q. v.).

hilip and Frances
Y WYAN, and had

PH LEONARD; and
MS, and had issue a
ie removed to England,
eth Tyson, who brought
S ELLICOTT. (q. v.)
MAS* engaged in the
i advanced age, leaving
, md. and has several
; JOHN, d. s p.; and
resides near London, and
IP W. THOMAS had
of whom one md. ——
and had issue: Philip
William Evan still liv-
louse of P. W. Thomas,

i and Ann (Chew)
l at Perry Point, on
Havre-de-Grace, and
n both sides of the
his cousin MARY,
wden) Thomas;

any account of this branch of
ive outline to Messrs. W. G.

William Alexander
b. Aug 26 1803.
. Dec 30. 1879.
m
na Bush.

John Wyan
b. Mar 11. 1860

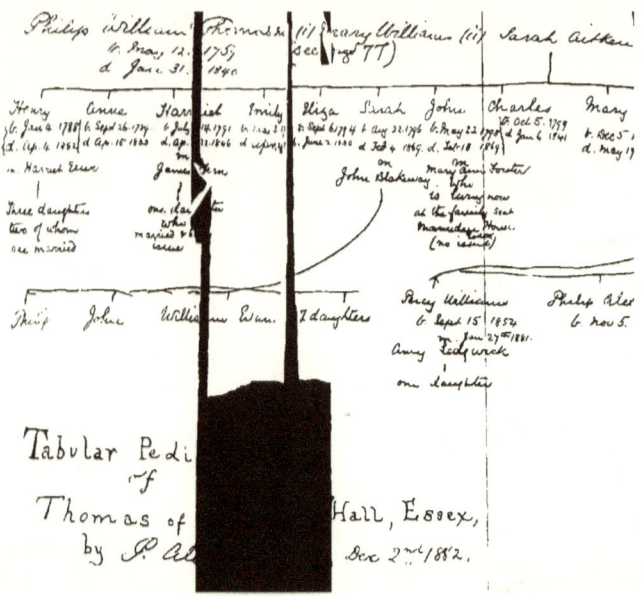

Philip William Thomas (1) Mary Williams (1) Sarah Aitken
b. May 12. 1755 (sec. pg. 77)
d. Jan. 31. 1840

Henry · Anne · Harriet · Emily · Eliza · Sarah · John · Charles · Mary
b. Jan 4 1789 · b. Sept 26. 1794 · b. July 16. 1791 · b. Nov 11 · b. Sept 6 1774 · b. Aug 22 1796 · b. May 22 1790 · b. Oct 5. 1759 · b. Dec 5
d. Ap. 4 1882 · d. Ap 18 1803 · d. Ap. 11 1846 · d. infancy · b. June 2 1800 · d. Feb 4 1869 · d. Feb 18 1869 · d. Jan 6 1841 · d. May 19
m. Harriet Essex · · · · · · · d. Jan 6 1841

m. James Thin · · John Blakeway · · Mary Ann Forster
· · · · · · is living now
Three daughters · one daughter · · · at the family seat
two of whom · who · · · Thursden House.
are married · married & · · · (no issue)
· · issue

Philip · John · William · Edwd · 7 daughters · · · Percy Williams · Philip Alec
· · · · · · · b. Sept 15 1852 · b. Nov 5
· · · · · · · m. Jan 27th 1881.
· · · · · · Amy Sedgwick
· · · · · · · one daughter

Tabular Pedigree
of
Thomas of   Hall, Essex,
by P. Al   Dec 2nd 1882.

SAMUEL d. i.; SARA
m. 1st Jany. 8th, 1702
2d July 30th, 1704 Tℎ
presently:

SAMUEL, only
(Harrison) Thoma:
Minister of the Soci
when he received a ce
Meeting, from West
May 15th, 1688, at :
County, MARY, youɪ
beth Hutchins, of
1751. He died before
SARAH b. March ˜
RICHARDSON (q. v.
SAMUEL, the 2nd, ℎ
March 1st, 1694, of whℴ
(q. v); ELIZABETH
RICHARD SNOWDEl
m. July 31st, 1718, J∢
the 3d, b. Nov. 12th,
EDWARD FELL, of
March 1743, leaving iss
m. after 1735, WILLIA

PHILIP, eldesℷ
Samuel and Mary
as, b. March 1st, 1
1st in March 1721, FR
HOLLAND, and h
by her: WILLIAM, ∢
presently. He marr
August 11th, 1724, Aℕ
of Samuel and Marɥ
and died November 2
his wife May 22nd,
SAMUEL b. June
1727, (q. v.); MARY

1748, HENRY HILL, and had issue: HENRIETTA MARGARET md. BENJAMIN OGLE, of Annapolis, who d. in July 1809, his wife in Aug., 1815. Mrs. HILL md. 2dly, Feby. 7th, 1760, ROBERT, son of John Pleasants, of Virginia, by whom she had issue: ANN THOMAS; ELIZABETH b. March 8th, 1732-3, md. SAMUEL SNOWDEN (q. v.); RICHARD b. July 17th, 1736, md. DEBORAH HUGHES, and had issue: PHILIP md. —— MYERS; and ELIZABETH md. STEPHEN STEWART, before Nov. 26th, 1777; JOHN b. Aug. 26th, 1743 (q. v.).

WILLIAM, only son of Philip and Frances (Holland) Thomas, md. MARY WYAN, and had issue:

MARY ANN md. Captain JOSEPH LEONARD; and PHILIP WILLIAM md. MARY WILLIAMS, and had issue a dau., HENRIETTA; soon after her birth he removed to England, leaving her with her cousins Isaac and Elizabeth Tyson, who brought her up, and at whose house she md. JAMES ELLICOTT. (q. v.) After his removal to England P. W. THOMAS* engaged in the Banking business in London, and d. at an advanced age, leaving issue: three sons, HENRY b. about 1768, md. and has several daughters, one of whom md. —— l'Ansen; JOHN, d. s p.; and WILLIAM ALEXANDER md. —— BUSH, resides near London, and has two sons, Percy and Alexander. PHILIP W. THOMAS had also several daughters, all now deceased, of whom one md. —— FERN, and another md. —— BLAKEWAY and had issue: Philip d. about 1871; John d. about 1860; and William Evan still living and the active partner in the Banking House of P. W. Thomas, Sons & Co.

SAMUEL, eldest son of Philip and Ann (Chew) Thomas, b. June 4th, 1725, resided at Perry Point, on the Susquehannah River, opposite Havre-de-Grace, and was proprietor of the Ferry rights on both sides of the River. He md. Oct. 23rd, 1750, his cousin MARY, dau. of Samuel and Mary (Snowden) Thomas;

*NOTE—Repeated requests have failed to obtain any account of this branch of the family from its present members. I owe the above outline to Messrs. W. G. Thomas and John Wethered.

who d. March 4th, 1770, and her husband d. July 17th, 1784, having had issue:

ANN b. Oct. 2d, 1751, md. THOMAS RUSSEL (q. v.); PHILIP b. Aug. 12th, 1753, d. s. p.; SAMUEL b. June 20th, 1757, d. May 20th, 1759; RICHARD SNOWDEN b Feb. 25th, 1762, of whom presently; JOHN CHEW b. Oct. 15th, 1764, (q. v.); SAMUEL b. Feb. 2d, 1776, was a Minister of the Society of Friends, md. Sept. 17th, 1789, ANNA, dau. of Dr. Charles Alexander Warfield, also a Minister of the Society of Friends, who d. May 19th, and her husband Oct. 1st, 1820, having had issue: ELIZABETH WARFIELD b. Nov. 14th, 1790, md. Oct. 7th, 1806, NICHOLAS SNOWDEN, (q. v.); HARRIET ANN b. Dec. 16th, 1793, d. Jan. 16th, 1794; and JULIANNA MARIA b. Jan. 16th, 1795, md. Sept. 24th, 1811, ISAAC KNIGHT, (q. v.); and EVAN WILLIAM b. Feb. 6th, 1769 (q. v)

RICHARD SNOWDEN THOMAS, eldest surviving son of Samuel and Mary (Thomas) Thomas, b. February 25th, 1762, resided at Perry Point, near Havre-de-Grace. He md. December 13th, 1784, MARY, only dau. of Sutherland Mifflin, and d. July 29th, 1814, having had issue:

SAMUEL b. Sept. 1st, 1785, d. s. p.; RICHARD SNOWDEN b. Jan 11th, 1787, d. s. p. April 23d, 1871; MARY b. June 25th, 1788, md. DAVID JONES, (q. v.); ANN b. Nov. 4th, 1789, d. Feb. 7th, 1793; JOHANNAH b. Nov. 16th, 1790, d. Oct. 13th, 1792; DEBORAH b. March 17th, 1792, md. GUSTAVUS WRIGHT, and had issue: GUSTAVUS; WILLIAM b. Aug. 8th, 1793, d. s. p.; ELIZABETH b. Jan. 25th, 1795, d. s. p; MIFFLIN b. April 11th, 1796, d. s. p. Oct. 9th, 1821; HENRY b. Sept. 15th, 1797, d. Aug. 28th, 1798; JOHN b. March 7th, 1799, of whom presently; HENRY EDWARD b. Jan. 1st. 1802, d. Sept. 11th, 1803,

JOHN, eleventh child of Richard Snowden and Mary Thomas, b. March 7th, 1799, md. in May or June 1826, HARRIET MARIA STRONG; he d. August 18th, 1837, and his wife January 7th, 1866, having had issue:

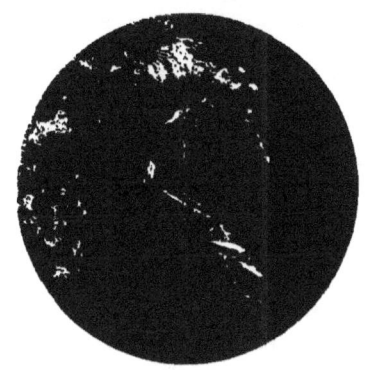

i.   MARY SUSANNA b. in May 1829, d. in Sept. 1829.

ii.   HENRY MIFFLIN b. April 1st, 1831, md. Nov. 27th, 1860, SARAH LOUISA CHAMBERLAIN, and has issue: MIFFLIN WILBUR b. Sept. 12th, 1861; ELLA CHAMBERLAIN b. May 7th, 1864; RICHARD SNOWDEN b. Jan. 23d, 1866; LAURA REBECCA b. Sept. 16th, 1867; JOHN ALEXANDER b. June 8th, 1874.

iii. JOHN EVAN b. Jan. 28th, 1834, md. Feb. 22d, 1865, LAURA CORNELIA TILDEN, and had issue: GEORGE HINES b. Feb. 23d, 1866; JOHN EVAN and HARRIET MAUD, twins, b. Nov. 7th, 1867, the former d. Aug 23d, 1868; and MARY MIFFLIN b. Dec. 12th, 1870.

iv.   LAWRENCE ALEXANDER b. March 6th, 1837.

JOHN CHEW, fourth son of Samuel and Mary Thomas, b. October 15th, 1764, resided after his marriage at "Fairland," in Anne Arundel County, which place he afterwards sold for $50,000. He was a man of high character, and birth-right member of the Society of Friends. In early life he took an active interest in politics and was elected by the Federal party in Maryland one of their Representatives in the Congress of 1799–1801. As a member of that House he took part in the celebrated election of President in the last named year, which, after three days of intense excitement, and thirty-five ballots, resulted in the election of Thomas Jefferson. On marrying an heiress and becoming a slaveholder, he lost his membership in the Society of Friends, but February 12th, 1812, he manumitted his slaves to the number of over one hundred and was received again into membership with the Society. He md. September 18th, 1788, MARY, only daughter and heiress of Richard and Eliza (Rutland) Snowden, of "Fairland," Anne Arundel County, Maryland, and died at his residence in Leiperville, Pennsylvania, May 10th, 1836. By his wife, who died November 13th, 1844, at the residence of her son, Dr. Richard H. Thomas, he had issue:

MARY ANN b. Jan. 23d, 1789, d. April 4th, 1790; ANN
SNOWDEN b. March 13th, 1791, d. Oct. 2d, 1791; ELIZA
SNOWDEN b. Aug. 8th, 1792, md. May 3d, 1810, GEORGE
GRAY LEIPER, of "Lapidea," (q. v.); SAMUEL b. March
28th, 1794, d. Sept. 14th, 1804; THOMAS SNOWDEN b.
Feb. 19th, 1796, of whom presently; JOHN CHEW b. Aug.
21st, 1797, d. March 15th, 1799; HENRIETTA MARIA b. July
30th, 1799, d. unmarried, Jan. 17th, 1874, at the residence of the
family of her brother, Dr. Richard H. Thomas, over whom
she had exercised a mother's care from the time of their own
mother's death; MARY SNOWDEN b. Sept. 22d, 1801, d.
Aug. 13th, 1802; Dr. JOHN CHEW b. Sept. 22d, 1803, (q.
v.); Dr. RICHARD HENRY b. June 20th, 1805, (q. v.);
SAMUEL EVAN b. March 12th, 1807, md. —— ——, and
d. in 1851, leaving issue: ANNIE, JOHN CHEW, and MARY
SNOWDEN; JULIA b. Aug. 16th, 1808, a Minister of the
Society of Friends, md. April 20th, 1845, BOND VALENTINE,
of Bellefonte, Centre County, Pa., a Minister of the Society of
Friends, who has since d. s. p.; HARRIET b. March 20th, and
d. March 27th, 1811; MARIA RUSSELL b. Aug. 29th, 1812,
d. in Nov. 1816; CHARLES b. Aug. 18th, 1816, d. in 1817.

THOMAS SNOWDEN, eldest son of John Chew
and Mary (Snowden) Thomas, b. February 19th,
1796, was at one time a member of the Legislature of
Maryland, md. December 31st, 1819, by Rev. Wm. Duke,
P. E. Minister of Elkton, Md., to ANN, dau. of William and Frances (Russell) Sewall. He resided at
North East, Cecil County, Md., where he died May 21st,
1857, leaving issue:

i.   Rev. JOHN CHEW b. Nov. 9th, 1820, a Minister of
the Methodist Episcopal Church, to which denomination his parents
belonged. He md March 16th, 1847, ANNIE HEATH WIL-
LIAMS, of Newton, Bucks Co., Pa., and died at Stroudsburg, in
the same State, leaving issue: NANNIE md. WM. HARMAR
THOMAS, (q. v.); GRIFFITH WILLIAMS b. Feby. 10th, 1853,
md. Feby. 10th, 1874, LIZZIE, dau. of Peter B. Melick, of
Philadelphia, and has issue: Mary, and Peter Brinton; and

FANNY BOSWELL md, in 1876, HUBERT LYON SMITH, of New Jersey.

ii. RUSSELL b. Aug. 7th, 1822, md. ELIZABETH A. MITCHELL, of Elkton, Md., and died April 22d, 1876, leaving issue: MARY ALICIA.

iii. NANCY b. Sept. 30th, 1824, d. unmarried in August 1873.

iv. FRANCES LOUISA b. Aug. 26th, 1826, md. April 8th, 1851, Rev. WILLIAM LAWS BOSWELL, a minister of the Methodist Episcopal Church, and at one time a Professor in Dickinson College. She died, after a short illness, April 17th, 1876, leaving issue: Rev. JAMES IVERSON, a minister of the Methodist Episcopal Church, b. Jan. 9th, 1852; THOMAS SNOWDEN b Nov. 6th, 1856; WILLIAM LAWS b July 18th, 1859; and RUSSELL THOMAS b. in Nov. 1863.

v. Rev. THOMAS SNOWDEN b. July 28th, 1828, a minister of the Methodist Episcopal Church, Chief Clerk of the Maryland House of Delegates 1860–61, and Hospital Chaplain U. S. A. 1862–65. He md. April 20th, 1854, ANNA M. MILLER, and has issue: JOSEPH MILLER b. Feby. 4th, 1855; MARY RUSSELL; ANN ELIZABETH; EMMA VIRGINIA; FANNY BOSWELL; HENRIETTA MARIA; and MARTHA.

vi. EVAN W. b. Sept. 13th, 1829, was a Lieutenant in the Maryland Volunteers, U. S. A., during the Civil War, md. June 2nd, 1866, MARTHA GRAY, dau. of Dr. Samuel Thomas, of Whitby Hall, and has issue: EVAN; ANNIE; and MARTHA.

vii. Rev. JAMES SEWALL b. Dec. 21st, 1831, a minister of the Methodist Episcopal Church, md. June 6th, 1863, EUNICE D. DRAKE, and has issue: EVAN WALDEN b. Feb. 26th, 1864; ANNIE HEATH b. May 3d, 1865, HELEN LOUISA b. Feb. 4th, 1867; THOMAS SNOWDEN b. March 17th, 1869; CARRIE RUSSELL b. Sept. 20th, 1871; and GRACE WILBUR b. Jany. 24th, 1874.

viii. MARY RUSSELL b. May 24th, 1825, d. Jany. 11th, 1849.

ix. ELIZA SNOWDEN.

Dr. JOHN CHEW, second surviving son of John Chew and Mary (Snowden) Thomas, b. Sept. 22d, 1803, at "Fairland," was graduated an M. D., at the University of Pennsylvania, April 8th, 1824. He was for some time in the Government employ at the building of the Newcastle Breakwater, and became a communicant of the Protestant Episcopal Church in that town; finally settled in Baltimore, Md., practicing his profession there. He was md. March 2d, 1848, by the Mayor of New York to JANE LAWRENCE, dau. of Thomas and Anna (Lawrence) Buckley, of that City, and died August 29th, 1862, leaving issue:

LAWRENCE BUCKLEY (the compiler of these "*Notes*") b. Dec. 6th. 1848, a clergyman of the Protestant Episcopal Church; JULIA b. March 9th, 1850, md. Oct. 14th, 1879, JAMES VALENTINE WAGNER; and WALTER WOOD b. June 11th, 1852.

Dr. RICHARD HENRY, tenth child of John Chew and Mary (Snowden) Thomas, b. June 20th, 1805, was educated at the University of Pennsylvania, sharing the first honors, and was graduated in its Medical School in 1828; afterwards he settled in Baltimore, where he had one of the largest practices; was a Professor in the Medical School of the University of Maryland, and an eminent Minister of the Society of Friends, in which capacity he traveled extensively in Europe and America. He md. first May 13th, 1830, MARTHA, dau. of Jas. Carey, a Bank President and distinguished Merchant of Baltimore, and had issue:

JAMES CAREY b. March 5th, 1832, d. i.; JOHN CHEW b. Jany. 3d, 1835, d. i; and Dr. JAMES CAREY, a Minister of the Society of Friends and practicing Physician, who md. Oct. 31st, 1855, MARY, dau. of John M. Whitall, of Philadelphia, and has issue: MARTHA CAREY; JOHN M. WHITALL; HENRY M.; BOND VALENTINE; MARY GRACE; MARGARET CHESTON; HELEN W.; FRANK S.; and DORA C.

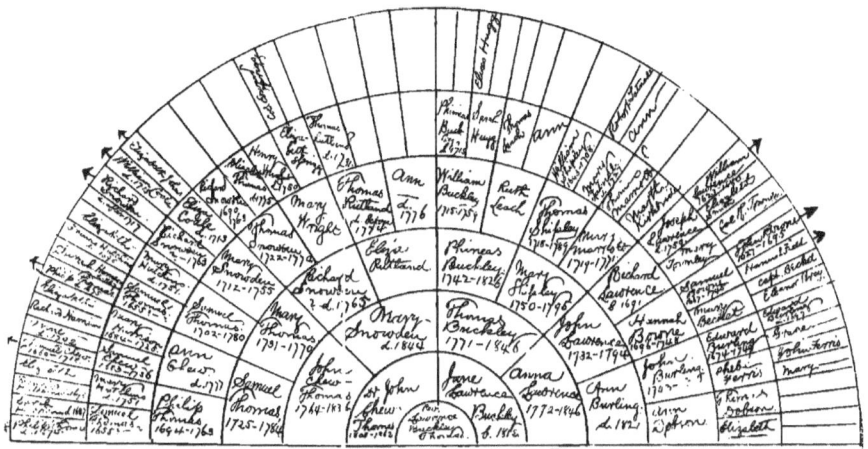

Ancestry of Rev. Lawrence Buckley Thomas,
as far as ascertained, Jany. 9th 1883.

Note. The figures show dates of birth and death, where they are known. The arrow heads, lines that cross the Ocean.

C
1!
U
s(
tl
o:
s(
B
t(
(]
2(

b.
J(
V
1]

C
1£
sł
S(
h(
tł
aı
ca
H
C
oі

'

b.
of
31
an
M
Hł

Dr R. H. THOMAS md. secondly February 9th, 1842, PHEBE, dau. of John and Phebe (Hicks) Clapp, of New York, and .had issue by her: JOHN CLAPP b. Dec. 11th, 1842; md. June 11th, 1873, EUGENIA, dau. of Richard Cromwell, of Baltimore; HENRY died in youth; ALLEN CLAPP b. Dec. 26th, 1846, md. Aug. 20th, 1872, REBECCA H., dau. of Russell and Phebe A. Marble, of Woonsocket, R. I, and has issue: EDWARD b. June 21st, 1877; and MIRIAM b. Sep. 14th, 1880; MARY SNOWDEN; CHARLES YARNALL b. Oct. 16th, 1851, md. Aug. 16th, 1877, REBECCA S., dau. of Joseph and Mary Edge, of Deer Creek, Md., and has issue: RICHARD HENRY b. Feb. 18th, 1881; and Dr. RICHARD HENRY b. Jany. 26th, 1854, md. March 1878, at London, Eng , ANNA LLOYD, dau. of Joseph Bevan Braithwaite, Barrister of that City, and has issue: HENRIETTA MARTHA b. May 24th, 1879.

Dr. R. H. THOMAS md. thirdly February 9th, 1859, DEBORAH C. HINSDALE, of New York City, a Minister of the Society of Friends, and died without further issue Jany. 15th, 1860.

EVAN WILLIAM, youngest son of John Chew and Mary (Snowden) Thomas, b. February 6th, 1769, md. January 5th, 1792, MARTHA, dau. of George and Martha Gray, of Whitby Hall, near Philadelphia, who d. February 9th, 1868; he d. August 27th, 1840, having had issue:

i. MARY b. March 15th, 1793, md. October 27th, 1810, Dr. GUSTAVUS WARFIELD. (q. v.)

ii. GEORGE GRAY b. December 28th, 1794, d. July 17th, 1795.

iii. EVAN WILLIAM b. May 22d, 1796, md. May 18th, 1826, ELIZA, dau. of Gen. Josiah Harmar, of Philadelphia, and d. s. p. at "Greenwood," near "Whitby," Sept. 17th, 1838.

iv. GEORGE GRAY b. Oct. 5th, 1798, md. first Sept. 29th, 1834, JANE H. GRAFF; second, ANN GRAY, dau. of Thomas and Elizabeth Leiper, of Philadelphia, who d. April

83

18th, 1881, and d. March 9th, 1854, having had issue: EVAN WILLIAM b. July 19th, 1835, d. Sept. 10th, 1860.

v.   Dr. SAMUEL b. July 20th, 1802, md. April 11th, 1832, HENRIETTA GRAFF, who d. in 1876, he d. Feb. 17th, 1864, having had issue:

i.   HENRIETTA md. June 7th, 1866, CHARLES EASTWICK.

ii.   WILLIAM HARMAR b. March 22d, 1845, resides at "Whitby Hall," md June 2d, 1870, NANNIE, dau. of Rev. John Chew and Annie Thomas, and has issue: Annie Heath; Julia Valentine; and Mabel Gray b. Sept 12th, 1880.

iii.   MARTHA md. June 2d, 1866, EVAN W. THOMAS. (q. v.)

iv.   EMMA md. June 2d, 1870, WILLIAM EASTWICK, and has issue: Lilly; and William, Jr.

PHILIP, second son of Philip and Anne (Chew) Thomas, b. July 3d, 1727, inherited from his father one-half of his estate at "Susquehannah Ferry," including "Mount Ararat" and extending from Perryville to Port Deposit, in all about 2,000 acres of land. He resided at West River, where he d. February 22d, 1784. He md. April 30th, 1754, ANNE, (Harris,) widow of Joseph Galloway, and had issue: an only son PHILIP,

This PHILIP THOMAS, Jun., lived at "Rockland," in Cecil County, and d. April 3d, 1809. He md. March 7th, 1782, at her father's residence, SARAH MARGARET, daughter of William and Catherine (Crumpton) Weems, of "Weemsforest," Calvert County. She d. July 22d, 1784, having had issue:

PHILIP b. Oct. 22d, 1783, (q. v.); CATHERINE b. Oct. 2d, 1785, md. May 1st, 1804, at "Rockland," GEORGE DAVIDSON, of the Eastern Shore, and d. leaving issue: Dr. JAMES P. md. ANN, dau. of Gov. Paca of Maryland, PHILIP md. MARY, dau. of —— Earle, and d. s. p., SARAH d. u, ELIZABETH md. BENJAMIN T. OWEN, FANNY d. u., and WILLIAM; ANN

WEEMS b. July 18th, 1787, after her sister's death, md. GEORGE DAVIDSON, as his second wife, June 2d, 1825, and d. leaving issue: CHARLES HENRY WHARTON, d. u, and JOHN MERRY-MAN md. —— ——, and has issue; JOHN WEEMS b. Jan. 27th, 1789, md Jan. 7th, 1813, ANN WEBSTER, of Baltimore; he resided near Port Deposit, Cecil County, Md., was manager of the Canal there, at one time member of the State Legislature, and d. about 1834, leaving issue: PHILIP md and has issue, and ELIZABETH WEEMS md. Rev. OWEN PATTEN THACKARA, of Florida; JAMES b. Dec. 20th, 1792, d. u. Nov. 27th, 1826; MARY b. April 15th, 1795, d. i.; WILLIAM b. Dec. 3d, 1796, d. i.; WILLIAM THORNTON b Nov. 3d, 1797, d i.; MARY FRANCES CAROLINE b. April 1st, 1798, of whom presently; CHARLES HENRY b. July 10th, 1799, d. i; BENJAMIN OGLE b. Nov. 5th, 1800, d. i; ELIZABETH ALICE b. Sept. 20th, 1802, d i; CAROLINE LOUISA b. Jan. 3d, 1804, d. i.; and GEORGE ARCHER b. Oct. 31st, 1805, md. HENRIETTA MARIA, dau. of Samuel Chamberlain, and d. leaving issue: NANNIE.

MARY FRANCES CAROLINE, the third dau. of Philip and Sarah (Weems) Thomas, b. April 1st, 1798, md. February 28th, 1828, JEREMIAH S. H. BOIES, of Boston, Mass., and d. May 30th, 1858, leaving issue: JEREMIAH S. b. Sept. 11th, 1831, d. u. Oct. 4th, 1858; JAMES THOMAS b. Dec. 26th, 1832, d. u. April 2d, 1859; SARAH H. b. March 31st, 1834, md. Sept. 28th, 1858, RICHARD F. A. PENROSE, M. D., LL. D., Professor in the Medical Department of the University of Pennsylvania, and d March 30th, 1881, having had issue: Boies b. Oct. 12th, 1859, d. July 20th, 1860; Boies b. Nov. 1st, 1860; Charles Bingham b. Feb 1st, 1861; Richard A. F. b. Dec. 17th, 1863; Spencer b. Nov. 2d, 1865; Francis Boies b. Aug. 2d, 1867; and Philip Thomas b. March 10th, 1869; and WILLIAM HUBBARD b. April 9th, 1836.

PHILIP, eldest son of Philip and Sarah Margaret (Weems) Thomas, b. October 22d, 1783, md. October 29th, 1807, FRANCES MARY, dau. of James and Elizabeth (Harrison) Ludlow, of New York City, and d. about 1848, having had issue:

i.   ELIZABETH FRANCES.

ii.   SARAH MARGARET md. SAMUEL TONKIN JONES, of Philadelphia, and d. leaving issue: FRANCES MARY md. RICHARD MONTGOMERY PELL.

iii.   CATHERINE ANN md. WILLIAM BRADFORD BEND of New York, who d. having had issue: WILLIAM BRADFORD md. ISABELLA TOMES; FRANCES LUDLOW d. y.; GEORGE HOFFMAN md. ELIZABETH TOWNSEND; KATHARINE ANN md. JAMES KENNEDY WHITAKER; ELIZABETH PELHAM md. HENRY A. ROBBINS; MARY LUDLOW; and FANNY d. y.

iv.   PHILIP WILLIAM md. Mrs. ANNA (ELLIARD) RAYMOND, and has issue: FRANCES MARY LUDLOW.

v.   MARTHA MARY md. as his second wife SAMUEL TONKIN JONES, and has had issue: SARAH MARGARET md. HENRY BEADEL; SAMUEL TONKIN, Jr., d. y.; SHIPLEY; and ELIZABETH LUDLOW md. JOHN DASH VAN BUREN, Jr.

vi.   LUDLOW md. MARY SMART THOMPSON, of Brooklyn, and has issue: MARY LUDLOW.

JOHN, youngest son of Philip and Ann (Chew) Thomas, b. August 26th, 1743, resided at West River, in Anne Arundel County, Md.; he was President of the Senate of Maryland; md. August 23d, 1777, SARAH, third child of Dr. William Murray, and d. February 3d, 1805, having had issue:

ANNE b. July 6th, 1778, d. in April, 1848, unmarried; PHILIP JOHN b July 29th, 1782, of whom presently; SARAH b. Oct. 28th, 1784, d. Oct. 12th, 1860, unmarried; JOHN b. April 27th, 1788, md. Dec. 31st, 1817, ELIZABETH, fourth dau. of Commodore Alexander Murray, of Philadelphia, and d. Dec. 27th, 1858; his wife is also d., having had issue: SALLY; JULIA MURRAY; ALEXANDER MURRAY, all unmarried and residing at "Lebanon," the family seat at West River; DANIEL MURRAY, an Attorney-at-Law of Baltimore City, and a prominent member of the Protestant Episcopal Church; MARY md. A. HAMILTON HALL, of West River, by whom she had two children; and CORNELIA, unmarried and resident at "Lebanon."

PHILIP JOHN, eldest son of **John** and **Sarah** (Murray) **Thomas**, b. July 29th, 1782, md. November 8th, 1804, **CORNELIA**, dau. of **Thomas Lancaster Lansdale**, and d. June 15th, 1859, having had issue: two daughters, MARY and CORNELIA; who both md. Dr. JAMES CHESTON; and a son, JOHN MOYLAN, of whom presently.

JOHN MOYLAN, only son of **Philip John** and **Cornelia** (Lansdale) **Thomas**, b. September 26th, 1805, practiced medicine in Washington, D. C., md. July 25th, 1829, **SARAH BROOKE LEE**, dau. of **Tench Ringgold**, and d. October 15th, 1853, having had issue:

MARY b. May 11th, 1830; ELIZA LEE b. Aug. 8th, 1831, d. u. in October 1865; JOHN MOYLAN b. March 2d, 1833, an Attorney-at-Law, of Philadelphia, Pa., md. October 24th, 1860, ADELE, dau. of Charles Ingersoll, of that city, and has issue: HELEN RINGGOLD b. Jan. 12th, 1862, CHARLES INGERSOLL b. Nov. 27th, 1865, and MARY GEORGINA LEE b. Sept. 9th. 1870; CORNELIA LANSDALE b. Sept 5th, 1834; LAWRENCE RINGGOLD b. in Sept, 1836; SAMUEL SPRIGG b. March 31st. 1838; SARAH BROOKE LEE b April 6th, 1840; ANNA MARIA b. Jan. 19th, 1842; WILLIAM LANSDALE b June 26th, 1844, d. in infancy; and CATHERINE LOUISA b. June 29th, 1845, d. i.

JOHN, the second son of **Samuel** and **Mary** (Hutchins) **Thomas**, md. in April, 1727, **ELIZABETH**, dau. of **Richard and Mary Snowden**, and d. in February, 1749-50, having had issue by his wife, who pre-deceased him:

RICHARD, of whom presently; SAMUEL, d. s. p.; ELIZABETH md. RICHARD RICHARDSON, (q. v.); JOHN b. in 1734, md. MARGARET HOPKINS, who died March 16th, 1806, aged 75 years, and her husbahd Feb. 15th 1826, without issue surviving.

RICHARD, eldest son of John and Elizabeth (Snowden) Thomas, b. about 1728, md. **SARAH COALE,** and had issue:

ARMS OF JOHNSON.

SAMUEL 3rd, b. Dec. 2nd, 1753, of whom presently; ELIZABETH b. Oct. 28th, 1755, md. ROGER JOHNSON, (q. v.); RICHARD b. Feb. 21st, 1758, (q. v.); JOHN b. Sept 27th, 1760, d. s. p. before Oct. 19th, 1781; MARY b. Mch. 12th, 1762, md. WILLIAM ROBERTSON, and had issue: SARAH md. JOSEPH HOWARD, (q v.), and THOMAS md. JANE B. BEVERLY; SARAH b. Nov. 26th, 1764, md. BERNARD GILPIN, (q v.); HENRIETTA b. February 17th, 1767, d. in infancy; MARGARET b. June 11th, 1769, md. GERARD BROOKE, (q. v.); WILLIAM b. Dec 11th, 1771, (q. v.); ANN b. May 25th, 1774, d. s. p.; and HENRIETTA, 2d, b. March 7th, 1777, d. s. p.

SAMUEL, eldest son of Richard and Sarah (Coale) Thomas, b. December 2d, 1753, settled in Montgomery County and md. October 31st, 1775, MARY, dau. of John Cowman, at her father's residence, and had issue:

SAMUEL b. Nov. 13th, 1776, of whom presently; JOHN 3d, b. Jany. 30th, 1778, (q. v.); SARAH b. Jany. 25th, 1781, md. WILLIS CANBY, and had issue: SAMUEL md. JULIET COCUS, and had issue: William T.; HENRIETTA b. Dec. 9th, 1782, md. CALEB BENTLEY, (q v); ELIZABETH b. April 28th, 1784, md. Oct. 13th, 1825, JAZER GARRETTSON, and d. s. p; and MARY b. Nov. 16th, 1785, md. JOSEPH HOWARD, (q. v.)

SAMUEL, eldest son of Samuel and Mary (Cowman) Thomas, b. Nov. 13th, 1776, md. MARY, dau. of Joshua and Rebecca (Owings) Howard, and had issue:

i.   REBECCA OWINGS b. Dec. 15th, 1797, d. s. p.

ii.   MATILDA BEAL b. Feby. 10th, 1800, d. s. p.

iii. MARY ANN b. Dec. 27th, 1801, md. 1st, CHARLES WORTHINGTON, and had issue: JOSEPH WILSON; and after his death md. 2d, JACOB SCHLEICH.

iv.   JOSHUA HOWARD b. March 2nd, 1804, md. 1st, LUCY COLSTON, and had issue: MARY ELIZABETH md. Dr. SAMUEL WATKINS; SUSAN MATILDA, 2d wife of Dr. SAMUEL WATKINS; LUCY HOWARD md. WILLIAM EDSON; ANN RE-BECCA md. her cousin, SAMUEL WALLACE THOMAS, (q. v.); VIRGINIA YOUNG md. ——— NALL; ALICE HENRIETTA md. JOHN G. CLOYD, of Decatur, Ill. JOSHUA H. THOMAS md. 2d. FANNY OWINGS, and had further issue: FANNY ZORAYDA md. SAMUEL ROBERTSON, of Elizabethtown, Ky.; and SAMUEL HOWARD.

v.   JAMES BAYARD b. Feby 4th, 1806, md. ELIZA-BETH J. A. GOODWIN, of Boston, Mass.

vi.   HENRIETTA ELIZA b. July 3d, 1809, md. WILLIAM HENRY BRIGGS, of Brookeville, Md. (q v.)

vii. SAMUEL BEAL b. Aug. 4th, 1811, of whom presently.

viii. SARAH CATHERINE b. Feb. 5th, 1814, md. THOMAS B. MUNFORD, and had issue: THOMAS SAMUEL b. in May, 1840, md. ETTA GUNTER; SARAH ELIZA b. in 1841, md. W. H. BRENTZ; ZORAYDA OWINGS md. J. W. MATTHIS; ANN AMELIA md. GEORGE BROWNFIELD; ELLEN BAYARD md. JOHN QWYMAN; and WILLIAM HENRY.

ix.   JOSEPH HENRY b. Feby 18th, md. AMANDA LA RUE, and had issue: WARREN LA RUE b. Jany. 25th, 1845, md MARY H. WARDROPER; MARY HELEN b. Aug. 16th, 1847, md. A. C. HODGES; ELIZA HOWARD b. Nov. 14th, 1849, md. CHARLES W. SWANSON; VIRGINIA BEAL b. Sept. 15th, 1851, md. SAMUEL V. LEIDOM; ANNA BROOKS b. June 27th, 1853; ELLA OWINGS b Sept. 26th, 1856; and WILLIAM BAYARD b. Feby. 14th, 1861.

x.   SUSAN AMELIA b. June 23d, 1821, md. JAMES

COX, and had issue: DAVID YOUNG; MARY THOMAS md. —— AYRE; ROLAND HUGHS; MEHETABLE; JAMES HENRY; BOYD; SAMUEL HENRY; ELI; and NANNIE.

SAMUEL BEAL, third son of **Samuel** and **Mary** (**Howard**) **Thomas,** b. August 4th, 1811, md. **ZORAYDA YOUNG,** who died in January, 1873, and her husband d. December 3d, 1874, having had issue:

JAMES HOWARD b. in 1836, d: in 1856; SAMUEL WALLACE b. in 1838, md. ANNA REBECCA, dau. of Joshua H. and Lucy Thomas, and d. s. p.; MARY LIZZIE b. in 1840, md. Col. JAMES B. PAYNE, of Elizabethtown, Ky., and had issue: SAMUEL THOMAS, LIZZIE ROBINSON, ELLA THOMAS, ZORAYDA YOUNG, EDWARD CHURCHILL d., SUSAN CHURCHILL, MARY and JAMES B. d., ELIZA C., and JULIA BLACKBURNE; ANN ZORAYDA b. in 1844; and ELLEN MATILDA b. in 1846, md. GEORGE W. WELCH, Jr., Cashier First National Bank, Danville, Ky., and has issue: ZORAYDA YOUNG, MARY BREATH, and SAMUEL THOMAS d.

JOHN, second son of **Samuel** and **Mary** (**Cowman**) **Thomas,** b. January 30th, 1778, md. —— **BERRY,** and had issue:

CHARLOTTE md WALTER GODEY, (q v.); NICHOLAS removed to Ohio, md. —— HIGGINS, and had issue: JOHN, MARY, NICHOLAS and WILLIAM; MARY; and CAROLINE, d. s. p.

ARMS OF BROOKE.

RICHARD, Jr., second son of **Richard** and **Sarah** (**Coale**) **Thomas,** b. February 21st, 1758, resided at Brookeville, in Montgomery County, Maryland. He md. **DEBORAH,** dau. of **Roger** and **Mary** (——) **Brooke,** who d. November 12th, 1814, and her husband November 6th, 1821, having had issue:

ELIZA P. b. Aug. 1st, 1874, d. u. aged 70 years; FRED-
ERICK AUGUSTUS b. Sept. 27th, 1788, d. Aug. 16th, 1794;
MARY b. October 18th, 1791, d. August 21st, 1794; SARAH
BROOKE b. April 26th, 1794, d. Sept. 25th, 1826; DEBORAH
b. March 2d, 1796, d. May 27th, 1797; MARGARET E. b.
March 3d, 1798, md. May 22d, 1816, ROBERT H., son of Wil-
liam and Hannah Garrigues, of Philadelphia, (q. v.); and
ROGER BROOKE b. April 9th, 1803.

WILLIAM, fourth son. of Richard and Sarah
(Coale) Thomas, b. Dec. 11th, 1771, md. MARTHA
PATRICK, and had issue:

ANNE POULTNEY b. April 14th, 1801, d. unmarried March
5th, 1830; ELIZA b. April 10th, 1803, md. WILLIAM HENRY
STABLER, (q. v.); MARIA R. b. Nov. 23d, 1804; HENRI-
ETTA b. Feby. 21st, 1807, d. Oct. 14th, 1821; RICHARD b.
April 19th, 1809, d. Oct. 15th, 1820; EDWARD b. June 22d,
1811, of whom presently; WILLIAM JOHN b. Sept. 15th, 1813,
(q. v.); SAMUEL PATRICK b. Jany. 23d, 1816, md. ELIZA
G. PORTER; JANE b. May 20th, 1818, md. CHARLES G.
PORTER; and MARTHA b. Feb. 3d, 1822, md. THOMAS P.
HARVEY, and had issue: GRACE, WILLIAM, CLARENCE,
EUGENE, and SWANN.

EDWARD, eldest surviving son of William and
Martha (Patrick) Thomas, born
June 22d, 1811, resides at "Ashland,"
in Montgomery County, Maryland.
He md. April 25th, 1833, LYDIA
S., dau. of Joseph and Sarah
Gilpin, and has had issue:

MARCELLA b. Feb. 13th, 1834, md.
in May 1853, ROBERT SULLIVAN;
RICHARD PIERCE b. Jany. 6th, 1836,
removed to Baltimore and engaged in Mercantile life, married September 29th, 1857,
HARRIET, dau. of John and Mary E. Cowman, of Alexan-
dria, Virginia, who was b. Dec. 17th, 1836, and has had issue:

ARMS OF GILPIN.

HERBERT b. Nov. 6th, 1859, MARGARET b. Oct. 25th, 1860, d. Oct. 7th, 1861, MABEL b. June 24th, 1862, d. Feby. 27th, 1865, HARVEY b. Aug. 5th, 1864, LOUISA b. Feby. 1st, 1867, and RICHARD HENRY b. March 12th, 1876; JOSEPH GILPIN b. Dec. 28th, 1837, d. July 7th, 1854; SAMUEL b. Jan. 21st, 1840, d. Nov. 22d, 1875; ALBAN GILPIN b. April 29th, 1843, md. Sept. 12th, 1871, SUSANNAH HAYDOCK, dau. of Thomas and Patience Leggett, of New York, and has issue: ANNA LEGGETT b. Dec. 3d, 1872, and HELEN LEGGETT b. June 2d, 1874; LOUISA b. Aug. 17th, 1845, md. September 14th, 1871, ROGER BROOKE, (q. v.); MARY PHILLIPS b. Dec. 8th, 1847; and EMILIE b. Sept. 6th, 1852, J. LLEWELLYN, son of John E. and Margaret A. Massey, of Virginia, and has issue: MARY GERTRUDE b. Dec. 7th, 1873, and MARGARET b. Aug. 10th, 1875.

WILLIAM JOHN, third son of William and Martha (Patrick) Thomas, b. September 15th, 1813, resides at "Clifton," in Montgomery County, md. REBECCA M. PORTER, and has issue:

MARY ELIZABETH b. Oct. 24th, 1838, md. WILLIAM WILSON, son of Robert Rowland and Hadassah Joanna (Townsend) Moore, of Sandy Spring, and has issue: CLARA PAINTER b. June 16th, 1860, d. August 8th, 1863, ROBERT ROWLAND b. April 15th, 1863, SARAH THOMAS b. Oct. 17th, 1865, REBECCA THOMAS b. July 9th, 1872; Dr. FRANCIS b. Jan. 30th, 1840, md. BEULAH L. HAINES, and has issue: WILLIAM FRANCIS b. June 21st, 1871, and ELLEN HAINES b. March 5th, 1875; SARAH .T. b. April 12th, 1841, md. Sept. 18th, 1862, BENJAMIN H. MILLER, and has issue:'REBECCA T. b. Feby. 1st, 1864, ELIZABETH T. b. August 13th, 1867, and MARTHA T. b. July 2d, 1870; EDWARD PORTER b. Jany. 16th, 1844, md. Nov. 30th, 1865, MARY HENRIETTA, dau. of Richard T. and Edith D. (Needles) Bentley, and has issue: EDITH BENTLEY b. Oct. 30th, 1866, MARY E. b. Feb. 28th, 1870, RICHARD BENTLEY b. Oct. 19th, 1873, EDWARD CLIFTON b. June 17th, 1875, and AUGUSTA NEEDLES b. June 12th, 1877; JOHN b. April 20th, 1846, md. in Nov., 1876, CATHERINE

D. VICKERS, of Baltimore, and has issue: EDNA V. b. August
28th, 1877; WILLIAM b. Aug. 20th, 1848, d. May 30th, 1871;
CHARLES b. August 3d, 1850; and MARTHA b. July 18th,
1852, md. in 1877, GRANVILLE FARQUHAR, and has issue:
WILLIAM JOHN THOMAS b. Sept. 8th, 1878, and FAITH b. in 1881.

SAMUEL, third son of Samuel and Mary
(Hutchins) Thomas, b. March 9th, 1702-3, md. Aug.
11th, 1730, MARY, dau. of Richard and Eliza (Coale)
Snowden, who d. August 15th, 1755, in her 43d year;
her husband d. February 3d, 1780, having had issue:

MARY b. November 3d, 1731, md. her cousin SAMUEL
THOMAS, (q. v.); SAMUEL b. September 23d, 1733, d. s. p.;
PHILIP b. April 18th, 1735, d. s. p. in Nov., 1754; ELIZABETH
b. March 10th, 1736-7, md. JOHNS HOPKINS, (q. v.); and
EVAN b. January 21st, 1738-9, md. Dec. 26th, 1766, at Indian
Spring Meeting House, RACHEL, dau. of Gerard Hopkins. Both
of them were Ministers of the Society of Friends, and persons of
a great deal of character. Before his death, EVAN THOMAS
freed his slaves, over 200 in number, and
gave them small allotments of land to
cultivate. He d. Nov. 10th, 1826, and
his wife Dec. 3d, 1825, having had
issue: MARY b. August 14th, 1768,
md. ELIAS ELLICOTT, (q. v.), ANN
b. August 6th, 1771, md. THOMAS
POULTNEY, (q. v.), PHILIP and
SAMUEL, twins, b. Jan. 12th, 1774,
both died in 1775, PHILIP EVAN, of
whom presently, ELIZABETH b. Mch.
26th, 1779, md. ISAAC TYSON, (q.
v.), EVAN, Jr., b. March 8th, 1781, d. s. p., and MARGARET
b. Sept. 26th, 1783, d. Oct. 5th, 1783.

ARMS OF POULTNEY.

PHILIP EVAN, third son of Evan and Rachel
(Hopkins) Thomas, b. at Mt. Radnor, in Montgomery County, Md., November 11th, 1776, was educated at
the District School, under a Mr. Knox, at Bladensburg.

Arriving at manhood, he went to Baltimore, then a town of only 15,000 inhabitants, and was received into the store of his brother-in-law, Thomas Poultney. In 1800 he commenced business on his own account, as a hardware merchant, on Baltimore Street, afterwards taking into partnership his wife's brother, Wm. E. George, and finally his brother Evan. He early took an interest in municipal affairs and public charities, and was the first President of the Maryland Bible Society, and the Mechanical Fire Company, one of the founders of the Baltimore Library Company, for many years President of the Mechanic's Bank, and advanced the first $25,000 to begin building the Washington Monument.

ARMS OF HOPKINS.

During the Fall of 1826 Philip E. Thomas had his mind directed to the loss which Baltimore had sustained by the diversion of a large part of its Western trade to Philadelphia and New York through the Erie Canal, and similar facilities for internal navigation and traffic in the States of New York and Pennsylvania. Gen. Barnard's report, showing the cost of completing the Chesapeake and Ohio Canal, and the difficulties that lay in its way, convinced him it would not accomplish the desired end in directing the Trade to Baltimore.

At this time Evan Thomas was in Europe, and wrote from England to his brother, giving him an account of the railroad just built from Stockton to Darlington, in Durhamshire, by the enterprise of Joseph Pease of the latter place.

Philip E. Thomas at once saw the utility of railroads as a means of communication and carriers of passengers and freight, and resigning his position as a State

P.E.Thomas

Director of the Canal Company, turned his whole attention to the projection of a railroad connecting Baltimore
with the West.

February 12th, 1827, twenty-five of the most influential Merchants of Baltimore met at the residence of Mr.
George Brown, pursuant to a call issued by Messrs.
Thomas and Brown. At this meeting Philip E. Thomas
ably presented the various advantages the railroad sys-
tem had over the Canal, and the old-fashioned turnpike,
in efficiency, rapidity of Carriage and ultimate economy,
and a committee was appointed to further examine the
subject, and report to a public meeting. This committee
consisted of Philip E. Thomas, Chairman, Benjamin C.
Howard, George Brown, Talbot Jones, Joseph W. Pat-
terson, Evan Thomas and John V. L. McMahon. The
following Monday, February 19th, the committee presented
their report, written by their chairman, which was unan-
imously adopted, and ordered to be printed and widely
distributed.

A charter for a Road having been obtained, largely
through the instrumentality of John V. L. McMahon,
and the proposed amount of stock speedily taken, and the
Baltimore and Ohio Railroad Company was duly organ-
ized April 24th, 1827, being the first one in America.

The first Board of Directors were: Philip E. Thomas,
President; George Brown,
Treasurer; Charles Carroll,
of Carrollton, William Pat-
terson, Robert Oliver, Alex-
ander Brown, Isaac McKim,
William Lorman, George
Hoffman, Thomas Ellicott,
John B. Morris, Talbot Jones
and William Steuart.

ARMS OF ELLICOTT.

A committee of Engineers was appointed to make
the necessary surveys for the route of the Road, con-

sisting of Colonel Stephen H. Long and Jonathan Knight, on the part of the Company, assisted by a number from the U. S. Topographical Corps; Philip E. Thomas being its chairman. April 5th, 1828, Messrs. Long and Knight reported the completion of their surveys, and choice of a route along the Valley of the Patapsco, and thence in the direction of Linganore Creek to the Point of Rocks.

July 4th, of the same year, the "first stone" was laid by Charles Carroll, of Carrollton, with great ceremony and a magnificent procession of Associations, Trades and Professions. Before the road passed four miles from the city, it encountered a high dividing ridge, which had to be cut down fifty-four feet through a hard clay, involving an expense far beyond the estimates, and the funds prepared to meet them. The President and nine of the Directors immediately advanced $20,000 apiece, which met the difficulty, and the road was completed to the Point of Rocks. Here it was delayed by the action of the Chesapeake and Ohio Canal Company, and it was not until after long and vexatious litigation that a compromise was effected.

In June, 1830, the road was opened for passenger travel as far as Ellicott's Mills; horse and mule power being used. Among other experiments in motive power tried during this first year, Evan Thomas constructed a car with sails, called the "Æolus," which attracted much attention, and a model of it was sent to Russia.

April 1st, 1832, the whole line was opened to the Point of Rocks. In 1831 it was decided to adopt steam as a motive power, and Locomotives replaced the horses and mules previously employed.

In 1833 the dispute with the Canal Company was adjusted, and the Rail Road was soon open to Harper's Ferry. June 30th, 1836, Philip E. Thomas, against the earnest remonstrances of the Board, resigned the Presidency of of the Company, being compelled to do so by the state of his health.

In one of the resolutions passed by the Board on this occasion they say: "On the commencement of this work, of which he has been, in fact, the father and projector, everything connected with its construction was new, crude and doubtful, with little to guide the, way, and that derived from distant and uncertain sources; now, such has been the increase of information and experience acquired under his auspices and direction, as to insure the completion and success of the undertaking, if prosecuted with the same zeal, assiduity and integrity which have ever marked his course."

Philip E. Thomas was a prominent member of the Society of Friends, of which his father had been an eminent Minister; was much interested in the cause of the Indians, several of their young men were educated at the same school with his sons, and it was owing to his exertions that the remnant of the Six Nations, residing in Western New York, were not driven from their Reservation by the intrigues of the Ogden Land Company with their chiefs. The chiefs were deposed, and a republican form of government established. He was afterwards made a chief of the Swan tribe of Seneca Indians, by the name of "Sagouan" or bountiful giver, and represented them in their intercourse with the government at Washington. In the summer of 1861, he went, as was his usual custom, to his daughter's, in Westchester County, New York, and died there September 1st, 1861.

He md. April 20th, 1801, **ELIZABETH,** dau. of **Robert** and **Ann (Edmundson) George,** of Kent Co., Md., and left issue by her:

ANN b. Feby. 17th, 1803, md. **THOMAS E. WALKER,** (q. v.); **RACHEL** b. February 1st, 1805, md. **J. J. WALKER,** (q. v.); **EVAN PHILIP** b. Nov. 19th, 1806, md. Nov. 17th, 1835, **ELIZABETH,** dau. of **Joseph** and **Eliza (Onion) Todhunter,** and d. leaving issue: **PHILIP WILLIAM** b. March 21st, 1842, d. July 14th, 1861, **KATE TODHUNTER** md. Dec. 24th,

1866, EDWARD GOODWIN DYKE, of Boston, and JOSEPHINE;
WILLIAM GEORGE b. Feb. 9th, 1809, of whom presently; MARY b. Oct. 11th, 1813, md. JOHN WETHERED, q. v.); ELIZABETH b. Jany. 22d, 1817; and HARRIET b. Oct. 25th, 1820, md. JAMES C. BELL, and has issue: PHILIP THOMAS, JOHN WETHERED, JAMES CHRISTIE, JACOB HARVEY and ELIZABETH

ARMS OF WETHERED.

WILLIAM GEORGE, second son of Philip E. and Elizabeth (George) Thomas, b. February 9th, 1809, was a prominent merchant of Baltimore, succeeding his father in the hardware business, on Baltimore Street. To him the City of Baltimore is indebted for her first improved public square, Franklin Square, in the North-western section of the City; her first charitable institution erected by private subscription, the Widow's Home, and her first line of Omnibuses. He married MARY LEWIN, dau. of Lewin and Elizabeth (Ellicott) Wethered, and has had issue:

ELIZABETH d. i.; PHILIP EVAN b. April 28th, 1834, of whom presently; ANN md. WILLIAM BELL, of New York, and has had issue: MARY LEWIN b. in 1855, REBECCA b. in 1858, d. in 1866, NANNIE b. in 1861, and ELIZABETH b. in 1871; LEWIN WETHERED b. in 1837, d. u. Dec. 8th, 1877; EVAN; MARY LEWIN md. in October, 1876, ALEXANDER SMITH, of New York, who d. s. p.; ELIZABETH md. CHARLES S. LINDSAY, and d. s. p.; MATILDA d. i.; HARRIET GEORGE, her twin sister, d. in 1866; and WETHERED BROTHERS md. Feby. 4th, 1880, ADDIE MELICK.

PHILIP EVAN, eldest son of William G. and Mary (Wethered) Thomas, b. April 28th, 1834, md. April 30th, 1859, MARIE SUZETTE, dau. of Mandeville de Marigny, whose father, Bernard de Marigny, of New Orleans, was a veteran of the war of 1812, and by birth a Duke and Marquis of France ; Miss de Marigny was also a grand daughter of William C. C. Claiborne. the first American Governor of Louisiana, and a great grand-daughter of Don Juan Ventura Morales, the last Spanish Governor of the Colony. Philip E. Thomas d. in January, 1882, leaving issue :

WILLIAMINE; PHILIP EVAN; MARIE SUZETTE; MARY LEWIN; MANDEVILLE DE MARIGNY; CLAIBORNE; and SOPHRONIE COALE.

TOMB OF RHYS AP THOMAS, K. G.
(St. Peter's Church, Caermarthen.)

NOTICES OF SIR RHYS AP THOMAS, K. G.

August 6th, 1494, Res ap Thom's Knyght Seals a deed with a square coat of arms having a raven between two flowering plants, over the raven the letter R. His Garter plate at Windsor has the motto "*Secret et hardi.*" This badge of a raven is a boss in the vaulting of the choir.

Sir Rhys' figure on his tomb at St. Peter's Church, Caermarthen (see the engraving) is recumbent in the attitude of prayer; in mail and chain armour, armorial bearings on the breast, with' the cloak and Collar of the Garter, head resting on a pillow, shield, helmet and lambrequin; the crest broken off just above the wreath; pillow, &c. curiously supported by the Dragon of Wales, lying on its back clasping the shield, his head issuing out of the wreath. At each top corner of the slab the arms are repeated. The feet rest against a couchant lion with his head twisted back. The figure of Lady Rhys is of small size in act of prayer, robes and cap temp. Henry VII. no animal at' the feet. See Topographer and Genealogist 1846, page 562.

Nicholas' County families of Wales Vol. I, 241, prints the letter of Sir Rhys to Richard III, evading his request to send his son as a hostage and pledging fidelity, to Richard.

Elias Ashmole's Institution, &c., of the Order of the' Garter, Folio 713 gives Sir Rhys' arms.

Anstis' Memorials of the Garter has notices of him Vol. I, 237, 238, 247, 264, 279, 292, 369, &c. A biography of Sir Rhys and notice of his ancestry may be found in Vol. I, of the Cambrian Register London 1796. I have never been able to see a copy of this rare volume.

I print his Will from the original at London.

"In the name of God. Amen. The thirde day of the moneth of ffebruary In the yere of our lord god a Thousande fyve hundred and xxiiij⁰ . I Sir Rys ap Thomas, Knyght of the order of the garter. hole of mynde and memory notwithstanding being syke in my body. And submyttyng my selfe unto the hands and mercy of the high omn'potent doo ordeyn and constitute my testament in thys forme folowing. ffirste I bequeth my soule unto almighty god, his meke mother mary and to all the blessid company of hevyn. And my body to be buried in the Chauncell of the gray freres of Kermerdyn there as my mother lyeth and whansoever it please god to call my wife out of this transitory lyfe my will is that she be buried by me. Item. I bequeth to the Cathedrall Churche of Sainct David xx⁰. Item to the ffreres of Kermerden xx⁰. Item to the Priory of Kermerden vi⁰ xiij⁰ iiij⁰. Item to the Rode Church at Kermerden a vestment price liij⁰ iiij⁰. Item to sainct Peter's Churche at Kermerden a vestment and a chaleis price v⁰. Item to sainct Barbara Chapell a vestment price xl⁰. Item to sainct Kustyd a vestment price xl⁰. Item to sainct Sadorn a vestment price xl⁰. Item to our lady of llan ll⁀w th a vestment price xl⁰. Item to our lady Church of llandivaison by Newton a vestment price xl⁰. Item to the freres of Brecknock liij⁰ iiij⁰ to bye a vestment before our Savyour Jesus. Item to the ffreres of Hau'ford West a vestment prc. liij⁰ iiij⁰. Item to the freres minors of hau'ford Est a vestment price liij⁰ iiij⁰. Item to the Abbey of Aidbure viij⁰ in money to bye a paire of Organs to honour god w t in the said Abbey. Item to our lady Chapell at the Bridge ende of Cothy a vestment price xl⁰. Item a crosse of silver to be made for the p'ishe Church of Carowe as my wife shall thinke good. Item I will that my wyfe during her lyfe n'turall shall enjoye all my londes in newe Kermerdyn and oulde Kermerdyn w t the ffraunches of the same which she is seased in, except suche howses as my doughter the lady Kateryn haward hath for th accomplisshement of her Joynto r. Item more I geve and bequeth to my said wife in money one hundred pounds, oon of the best basyns an ewer, a standinge Cupp gilt w t all the plate that cam to me from maister John Griffith. Item more to my said wife xij fether bedds with ιth appurten'nces with ij hangings of silke xij paire of shets xij borde clothes, four doseyn napkyns and xij towells. Item I will that my said Wife enioye the thirde part of all my lordshipps and lands I have during her said lyfe except suche londes as my said doughter the lady haward hath for her joynto r as is aforesaid. Item I will that all my plate be weyed and valued to the uttermost except suche plate as I have before bequeathed to my wife. And that my sonne Rys Griffith sett owt as moch money as my said plate will draw to. to mary his sister Elizabeth and ouer that to geve wᵗ her asmoch as he shall thinke good yf she will be ordred by hym. Item I geve and bequeth unto my Baase sonnes all my Catall as Oxen. Kyne shepe and Kothiis. To be devided betwene them as by the ouerseers of this my testament shallbe thought goode trusting that they will consider that those which be (not?) maried to have more to their porcions than they that be maried and hath somewhat alredy. Item I geve and bequeth unto eu'ery houshold serv'nt of myn their hole wages for oon yere. And will that their horses and harneys remayn wᵗ them and not to be taken from any of theym. Item I will that fyue poundes in londes be surely founded to the gray freres of Kermerdyn for a Chauntry there to fynde two prests to pray for me and my wife forever. Item I geve and bequeth to the overseers of this my testament to se my will p'fourmed for their payne an labour xxˡˡ. The Residue of my goodes and catell not bequethed I geve and grannt to my sonne Ris Griffith whom I do ordeyn and constitute to be myn executour through th advice of the right honourable and mighty prince the Duke of Norffolks grace. So as my said sonne may ordeyn and dispouse the same as he shall think goode unto the pleasure of almighty god for the welthe of my soule   Moreover I doo ordeyn and constitute to be overseers of this my will and testament my lord pryour of Kermerdyn, Doctour John Vaughan, Maister lloid Chaunter of sainct David, Maister Stradling, Chauncelor of the same, Maister Lewis Griffith, William John ap Thomas, Thomas John's, David Lloid, Lewis Thomas ap John and howell ap Ridderch. Witnesse beinge present att the making herof Doctour David Mathvey, wardeyn of the gray ffreres of Kermerdyn, Maister John Lewis, Tresorer of sainct David, Jem'i (?) Lloid, &c &c, with all the overseers aforenamed and many others."

Proved in the Prerogative Court of Canterbury, July 5ᵗʰ, 1525.

103

Sir Griffith ap Rhys K. B. only son of Sir Rhys ap Thomas K. G.; md. in 1504, Katherine, dau. of Sir John St. John. At the funeral of Prince Arthur a contemporary account says:

ARMS OF ST. JOHN.

"Sir Griffith Vap Sr. Ris rode before the corpse in mornyng Abitt on a courser trapped wth black bearing banner of Prince's arms."

And at Worcester, "Sir Griffith Vap Rise Thomas offerred at the Gospel the rich embroidered banner of my Lord's Armes." The standard of Sir Griffith ap Rhys K. B. was: per fess murrey and blue, device, repeated twice a trefoil slipped and barbed argent, charged with a raven proper. Motto. "Pullis corvorum invocantibus eum" Psalm cxlvii, 9. (See Grose's Antiquarian Repertory, Vol. II., 327, 330.)

Sir Griffith Ryce son to Sir Rhys ap Thomas Knight deceased Sept. 29' of the 14th year of Henry VIII. See inscription on his tomb and engraving of it. Thomas' Antiquities of Worcester S. 71.

Notices of Sir Griffith ap Rhys may be found in the' Calendar of State papers of Great Britain, Reign of Henry VIII., Vol. II., 69, 193, 235, 245, 410, 967, 1097, 1357, 1454, 1489, &c.

COPY OF A LETTER FROM SIR RYS GRIFFITH
TO CARDINAL WOLSEY.

Pleasith it yo r most reuerende fatherhod And my moost singuler good lorde and maister to call to your good and noble remembraunce howe it pleased the same yo r moost noble grace of yo r goodness and benigne favour to me shewed to gyf me Incomaundement when I or anny my pouer s'vants or tenants shulde have anny Wrong to make relac'on thereof to

'Aedd Mawr,'
Prydain
Dyfnwarth Hen
Dyfnwal Moelmud (the Lawgiver)
3 Beli 4 Bran
Gwrgant Varvdrwch. B.C. 650.
Euhelyn B.C. 636 = Marcia d. B.C. 600.
Siteyllt
Cerinvath Cyan
Morryd,
Gorwynion, Arthal, Peredur, Elydnog.
Rhun Geraint
7 Cadell B.C. 500.
Coel
Por
Geraint
Andryw
Urien

2 Ithel
Lydog
Lydno
Forust
Meirion
Blaiddyd, B.C. 266.
Offa B.C. 263.
Owain
Siseyllt 2d.
Arthvael
Sidal
Rhodawt
Rhydderch
Sgol Benisel
Fernex Portrex
Cai
Manogan d. B.C. 100.

Beli Mawr d.B.C 60
8 Lludd Cassallon or Cassibelaunus
Ephranwy
Eiddilen
Ennos Asclepiodotus
Einydd
Eudeyrn
Euddigant
Rhuddeyrn
Rhwg Ivrdel
Gradd
Urben
Tudbwryl
Deheuvraint
Tegvan
10 Coel Godebawg
St. Ceneu "St. Helena" B.D. 330 b 248 d. 328
Cedlym
Gwrwost
Merchion Gul

Dyno ... Cor ... Kenyn dau ...
Urien Rheged and Morganane Eurdoyl and Elidyr
Pasgen Owain ap Arthur
Elwin
Mor md. Morgan Morganwr
Rhyne
Sysoylt
Gurwared
Kymbathurse
Lloarch
Pinoin
Goronurg
Rhys = Margaret dau S heir
Rhys
Elider = Gladys's
Sir Elider ...

Traditional Pedigree
of Sir Rhys ap Thomas K.G.   No I.
Principally from Welsh authorities; compiled by Rev. Lawrence Buckley Thomas

ma
_____

lau. of

dau. of
= Dau
Ca
⌐
Wisley
⌐ mar
ith ef

st Eliza
dau. H

up Hou
ffet.
═ 1
═ 2
═ 3°

John
Fletsh
m Kn.
Howa
2°. Sir,

'Aedd Mawr,'	Itel	Beli Mawr d.B.C 60	13 Bryn ... Dav = Nevyn dau. of Brychan
Prydain	Eydog	Lludd Cassallon	12 Urien Rheged
Dyfnwarth Hen	Gydno	Caswallon or	md. Inorayane Eurdryl
Dyfnwal Moelmud The Lawgiver	Orwst	Evigbury Cassibelaunus	Can? md. Eluoyr
3 Beli 4 Bran	Neiron	Enddolan	Pasgen Owain ap Arthinis
Gwrgant Varvdrwch. B C 650.	Rauddyd	Ennos	Mor Elvri md. Morgan
Cuhelyn B. C. 636 = Marsia d. B.C 600.	Efo B C 266.	Evigdd	Asclepisdus
Sitsyllt	Dain	Eudeym	Rhyne
Cynwrach Dan	Sitselt 2 d.	Enddigant	Sysyllt
Morryd,	Alwall	Rhuddeym	Gurwared
Gorwynion. Arthal. Poredur. Elydnog	Idal	Rhudivedel	Kymbathurje
Rhun Geraint	Ridawr	Gradd	Lloarch
7 Cadell B. C. 500.	Ridderch	Eryrben	Simon
Coel	Sol Benisel	Tudburyl	Goronury
Por	Ferp Porrex	Dehewvraint	Rhys = Margaret dau. & heir
Geraint.	Cai	Tegvan	Rhys of Griffin ap Kildy
Andryw	Manogan d. A C 100.	10 Coel Goethebawg	Elider = Gladys dau. & heir
Urien		St. Eneu "St. Helestu d. A D 330 b 248 d. 328	of Llais ap Gul
		Redlym	Sir Elider ap Jorath Vrech
		Gwrwst	Dolu Lord of Seginbrath
		Merchion Gul	

Traditional Pedigree
of Sir Rhys Ap Thomas K. G. No I.
Principally from Welsh authorities; compiled by Rev. Lawrence Buckley Thomas

your grace. Accordyngly pleas ith it the same so it is that my pouer tenants and s'vants by the hight of malicious my'des of such light p'sons that be deputies under my lorde fferrers in these p'ties be dayly withowt cause reasonable or good grounde put to vexac'on and trouble wrongfully and some of my household s'vants kept under apparence from Countie to Countie ffor their pleasures only. And because that my lorde fferrers hym self is verry good unto me I were lothe to shewe the uttremost of their demean's towarde me and myn. In consideraꞇ'on whereof I moost humbly beseech youre moost noble grace that it it may pleas the same to be so favorable goode lorde unto me as to directe yo ͬ hon ͬ able l'res (letters) to the said lorde ferrers. Willing and desiring hym that I may be his deputie Justice and Chambr'layn in this p'ties the princypalitie of Southe Wales ffyndyng sufficient sureties to discharge hym ageynst the King's g'ce. And all other conc'nyng the exerceysing of the same his office And by cause the moost part of my power levyng is in the Auctorities And to have my pouer ten'a'ts and s'vants w ᵗʰ other my frynds in quiet And to leve in Rest my self so that I and they moght be the more able to do yo ͬ grace s'vyce. I wolde be contentyd so it myght stande withe yo ͬ g'ces pleasure to gyf my lorde such some or somes of money — as youre g'ce shulde thinke conson'nt — ou ͬ and abcue all the ffee or wage belongyng to the same his offices to be unto hym payed yerely without charge. And as I am bounden of verey duetie the uttremost since that end maye lie in my litle power your noble grace shal be assured p' f. As Knowith the blessed trinitie whoeur p'sve yo ͬ moost noble grace from all adv'sities.

ffrom Cayrewe the iijᵈ day of this m'the. (March, 1528–9)

Your humbell se'vante.

R s Griffuth

From the original in the Domestic State Papers.
(Record Office).

· ————

COPY OF A LETTER FROM DÁME KATHERINE RYS TO CARDINAL WOLSEY.

Right excellent father under God m' hitt please yo ͬ most habundant fatherhode hit is so that yo ͬ s'vant maist' R' gruffyth is in Warde in the Castell of Kerm'dey'n under the keping of the lorde fferrariis w ᵗ out any cause resonable for yo ͬ seid s'vant beying in the seid Castell bes'd ᵃ the

105

seid lorde fferrariis desiring oon Thomᵃ ap Owen s'vant unto the King's
honorable grace being in ward in the said castell bes'dᵉ the seid lorde
fferrariis desiring oon Thomᵃ ap Owen s'vant unto the King's honorable
grace being in ward in the said Castell surmising on the seid Thomas
ap Owe' that he shold tak on Jankyn s'vant unto yᵉ seid maist' Rs'
from the co'stable of the Castell of Kerm'dey'n wᵗ force the wᶜʰ is
not soe for ther be sufficent p'ves to the co'trary. wheropo' the said lord
ferers beying in his chambʳ wᵗ in the Castell of K. drewe his dager upo'
yoʳ seid s'vant and so yʳ s'vant in his defence drewe his dager but thankid
bee God ther was no harme don sav only yoʳ seid s'vant was hurt in his
arme by the seid lord ferers w'upo' the seid lord ferers com'dded yoʳ seid
s'vant on p'ey of mˡⁱ and apo' his almen (?) that he sholde not dep't owt of
the seid Castell newthelesse the co'tre is not co'tented yᵗ yʳ s'vant shold
remayn i' the seid Castell wherin yoʳ s'vant as yet hath kept all things as
yet in rest and peace and will do the best to do the same howbehit I fere
he will not be abill to kepe the i' rest and also hit was so yᵗ yoʳ seid
s'vant befor his comying to Kr'm'ddy' sent his s'vants to take a certy'
lodging in K. amongst his tenants for hym and (for?) alle gentillme' that
cu' wt' hy' and so sett up his armes upo' certey'n dores wʳ upo' the seid
lorde ferers s'vants i' contin'et of his comyng to Kerm'dyn toke downe
yᵉ seid armes fro' the dores wᵗ wᶜʰ the contre was not cont't wʳ for yoʳ
seid s'vant had great labor to cause the co'tre to be con'te'ted at yᵗ tym.
And alle was by cause he wode not offende the King's lawes and to kepe
yoʳ graciuse com'dment and besides hathe be'g a doyng en' sythe my lord
f'rers was officer in this p'ties for he and his officers hath be'on quareling
on all such snath and 'tend'th that was longing to yoʳ seid s'vant and all
things yᵗ he and his officers dose is lawe whether hit be right or wrong
My lord yoʳ s'vant wold have wrytten unto yoʳ grace but he was so kepte
that he had no plac to wrytt. My lord I besech yoʳ grace to be graciose
lord unto my husband and me for the great love that was bettwene yoʳ lordship and my lord my father and that yoᵘ will not suffʳ us to have no shame
nor rebuke for we have no trust but only in yoʳ gracious lordship for yoʳ
lordship shall have those that will sey the worst and not the best I be-
seche yoʳ grace to p'don me of my (relute?) wrytting for hit is my hast
and th'n p'sue yoʳ most habu'dant grace and long lyfe and do for us.
Wrytt'n at Kerm'dyn the xvii daye of Junii (1529)

by yeouᵣ pooer bed'wom'an

Katherne Rys.

CAREW CASTLE.
(Seat of Rhys ap Thomas, K. G.)

ARMS OF HOWARD OF EFFINGHAM.

March. 26. 1529 or 1530. (the year is uncertain. the Editor of the Calendar gives the former date,⁺ but I prefer the latter as more in accordance with the other notices of the affairs of Rice Griffith.) William Brabazon and Hugh Whalley write from Carew, they are there preparing for the safe conducting of the King's stuff. (apparently after the attainder) A chaplain of my Lady Howard's came with the King's command about her jointure and asked leave to lie in the castle that he might have the rooms cleaned. Suspected and searched his room and found four boxes of evidences belonging to Narberth, Carew, and Kidwelly. Among other things a silver Raven worth £40 .0 .0d. See Calendar of State papers reign Henry VIII, Vol. IV, 2372. Other notices connected with the Arrest of Rice ap Griffith may be found in the same Volume. 1962, 2281, 2356, 2362, 2511, 2512, 2519, 2572, 3021, 3024, and in Froude's History of England.

SUNDRY NOTICES OF THE NAME OF THOMAS;
IN THE CENTURY BEFORE A. D. 1651.

Nicholas' Wales. 616. John Thomas Bevan, Portreeve (or Mayor) of Swansea. 1604.

Ditto. 647. Thomas ap Evan of Eglwysilan d. 1612 son of Evan ap Meuric d. 1572 had a son Evan ap Thomas b. 1581 d. 1666. He md. Catherine dau. of Edward Lewis of Llanishen and had issue: Thomas b. 1615 (whose son adopted the surname Thomas)

Burke's Commoners III. 266 Rees of Killymaenllwyd descends from the uncle of Thomas ap Nicholas.

Burke's Ext. & Dormant Baronetage. Edward Thomas of Mitchellstown Glamorganshire Wales was made a Baronet Mch. 3. 1641-2. had a son Edward of whose descendants nothing is known.

Deacon's History of James Naylor was printed "London for E. Thomas, and are sold at his house in Green Arbor, 1657."

Whitaker's answer to Rainoldes was printed by Thomas Thomas, University of Cambridge, 1585.

Abel Thomas master of the "Swan" of Lyme Oct. 3. 1628 Abel, of Southampton on a voyage to Newfoundland. Apl. 24. 1637, with John Hallett owner of the "Swan" of Lyme & the "Goose" Oct. 17. 1629 S. P. D. Daniel, a Captain in Ireland Feby. 5. 1650. David, was of Llanwrystyd Co. Cardigan June. 19. 1634; David, fined £200 by Star Chamber Apl. 18. 1638; S. P. D. Edmund, of Molton, Co. Glamorgan distressed for tithes £7.0.0 in 1656. (Besse's Sufferings of Quakers 737) Edward, Warden of Free School, Wolverly Co. Worcester, June 18. 1635. Edward, opposed collection of Ship money in Co. Merioneth Mch. 10. 1636. Edward, of St. Albans to be arrested for inciting a mutiny June 1. 1649. S. P. D.

Royal Attorney General to decide whether Rose (Roos) wife of Richard Brest or Bridget grandmother of Elizabeth (Roos) Thomas is next heir to Robert Roos of Igmanthorpe York. Oct. 11. 1638. S. P. D. This Elizabeth md. before 1635 William Thomas of Essex and her grandmother Bridget wife of Peter Roos was dau. of Robert Roos aforesaid whose grandmother Alice was sister & Coheir of the last Lord Scrope of Upsale. See Nicholls' Coll. Top. et Gen. Vol. VIII. 163.

Thomas pedigrees of varying lengths may be found in Hasted's Kent ii. 243, 382; Berry's Sussex, 290, 299.

Berry's Kent, 416; Visitation of Middlesex. 1820. 44; Maclean's Trigg Minor, i. 305, ii. 171. 174; Gage's Thingoe Hundred, Suffolk, 359; Dallaway's Sussex, II. i. 44. 187; Harleian Society IX, 215: Hoare's Wiltshire, I. ii. 261; Meyrick's Cardigan, 160; Nicholas' County families of Wales, 952 &c.; Genealogist iii. 312; Phillipps' Glamorganshire Pedigrees, 7. 13. 14. 22. 33. 34. 40. 41, Do. Caermarthenshire Do. 66; Do. Cardiganshire Do. 114; Lewis Dwynn's Visitations of Wales, i. 47. 58, 60. 125. 159. 192. 201. ii. 133. 151. 190. 271. and Harleian Mss. Vol. IV. 412. Harleian Roll. C C 9. Charter Catalogue V. iii. These three at the British Museum.

Record Commission of Great Britain. Proceedings in Chancery i. 48 &c·; ii. 522; iii. 137 &c. and iv. 96 &c. contain sundry notices of the name see the indices. Calendarium inquisitiones post mortem. iii. 272 Ricus Thomas, armiger, held lands, woods & pastures at Hengstrig and at Heuston, Somerset, Anno. 2d. Henry IV. William Thomas had land grants temp. Henry VIII. see Jones Index to the Records. Mr. Thomas, Resident from England to Scotland 1525-6 T. S. Thomas' Historical Notes. 1069. Lewis Thomas Abbot of Kyme some·time between 1521-1540 Lansdowne Mss. 979. Robert Thomas made his Will in 1532. Cotton Mss. Vitellius, A. XVI. 209. b.

Calendars of State Papers, Domestic, published by the Master of the Rolls, England. Admiral Sir Thomas Button, answering charges against himself defends (his nephew) Captain William Thomas against the allegation of having tortured the gunner of the St. John of Dunkirk. March. 1634. Numerous notices of this Capt. Thomas may be found in the State Papers. Another William Thomas in a petition Apl. 16· 1634 says he has been at sea since 1617 Purser in the "Antelope" since 1625. Philip Thomas, Thomas Lawrence & Martin Sanders give information about a Romish plot. Apl. 1. 1628. Thomas ap Evan of Caron Co. Cardigan accused to Court of

High Commission Oct. 30. 1634. John Thomas and others, owners of the "John & Mary" of London July 3. 1634. John Thomas, purser of the "Moon" to be purser of the "Lion's 4th Whelp,". (his petition of Sept. 6 sets forth his services) Nov. 4. 1634. John Thomas Mayor of Bideford, Co. Devon Feb. 20. 1636. William Thomas, Purser of the "Swallow" Feb. 19. 1635. Capt. John Thomas, Master Gunner 1586. John Thomas of Romney concerned in smuggling wool 1577. Richard Thomas of Spergerwere tenant of Wm. Carnsew May. 2. 1569. William Thomas, Messenger from the Queen's Ambassador at the Emperor's Court June 17. 1558. John Thomas recommended to be a Purser Apl. 14. 1627. —— Thomas a solicitor dwelling in Chancery Lane over against the Rolls, London Feb. 21. 1632. William Thomas & others own the "Gift of God" of Newport, also the "Francis" Sept. 1. 1629. Walter Thomas had resigned as Muster-Master of Co. Pembroke June 14. 1630. Rice Thomas, gunner of the Tenth Lion's Whelp June 6. 1632 to be replaced by John Mears, gunner's mate. Rice's petition of May 8. 1633 gives his wife's extreme sickness as reason for his absence when the ship sailed. July 8' 1637 he was released from Prison where he had been two years for being short 9 barrels of gunpowder, which charge he denied. Was restored as gunner of the Tenth Whelp Nov. 29. 1637 Mark Thomas, Mayor of Rye, Dec. 14. 1638. William Thomas, Carpenter, values lead at Conway Castle, Aug. 12. 1636. Thomas Thomas of St. Martin's in the Fields London, Tailor, bond with two others for £1000. May. 14. 1636. Mary Thomas petitions about an annuity due her by Thomas Payne, a printer, "She and her husband aged and poor" Jany. 20. 1640. Richard Thomas *late* Mayor of Caermarthen Jany. 20. 1638. Philip Thomas at the Castle Tavern in St. Clements, London said of Prynne, Bastwick and Burton, "the punishment they had (ear cropping &c.) was not more than they deserved." Before Jan. 2. 1638.

Philip Thomas, Messenger of Commission for charitable uses suggested a new commission Aug. 13. 1638. Philip Thomas petitions East India Co. for wages. His behaviour is complained of ·and he is discharged Co.'s service Dec. 17. 1621. John Thomas minor, has presentation to Rectory of Llangan, Diocese of Llandaff Oct. 29. 1639. Nicholas Thomas of St. Mawes Co. Cornwall, Merchant reported worth £2000 Feb. 5. 1639. Rice Thomas of Biston Co. Monmouth, husbandman, Dec. 3. 1638. Warrants to Philip Thomas, Messenger of the Chamber, Sept. 18. 1638 William Thomas, Master of the "Mary" of London, June 23. 1640, Richard Thomas, bell-ringer at Whitehall Oct. 24. 1649.

Besse's Sufferings of the Quakers. London. 1753 i. p. 737 Edmund Thomas of Molton Glamorgan distressed for tithes £7. in 1656; p. 758. Evan Thomas in Pembrokeshire was fined for absence from Church; p. 41. Margaret Thomas was committed to Newgate prison Bristol for bearing testimony in Church in 1656; p. 65. Mary Thomas aged 65 in Bridewell, Bristol in 1681, also Margaret Thomas.

John Thomas, Captain of the Marigold one of Drake's Squadron, lost at sea in the Straits of Magellan, Sept. 30. 1638, the vessel drifting and never after heard from. Evan Thomas, Deputy Searcher of the Custom House under the Collector of Customs at Ipswich, Sandwich, Chichester & Southampton in Feby, 1591.

Calendar of State Papers Colonial. East Indies. Henry and Elizabeth Thomas petition for estate of Wife's deceased husband Jany. 16. 1624. Philip Thomas petitions for his half-brother John Stacy's estate Mch. 26. 1624. Philip Harrison factor at the Moluccas in 1624.

Nicholas' Battle of Agincourt. app. 24. Stephen Thomas Master of La Trinite' Royale (Ship) recovers an annuity of £6.13.4 in 1417

Histoire Genealogique &c. de la Maison Royale de France Paris 1726. Honore' de Thomas of Provence md. in 1552 Anne de Vintimille dau. of Melchior, Compte de Marseilles. Nicholas Thomas, Chevalier, was Master falconer to the King Nov. 48. 1371. Others of the name may be found in Vols. II. IV. V. VI. & VII.

More'ri grand dictionnaire Historique etc. X. 157 says the House of Thomas in Provence is one of the most noble, and gives a pedigree beginning in 1096. Arms: Ecartele' de gueules et d'azur 'a une croix pommettee' ou fleuronee', au pied fiche' d'or brochant, sur le tout.

Annales Monastici, Registrum Abbatiae Johannis Whethamstede. Reginald Thomas resigns the Rectory of Cameltone in Bedfordshire June 10. 1462

William Thomas Esq. of Swansea, Sheriff of Glamorgan 1644. James Thomas was Chester Herald in 1595. Philip Rhys ap Thomas was Mayor of Caermarthen in succession to Sir Griffith Rhys. Nicholas Wales. 267.

Evan Thomas ap Evan Under Sheriff of Glamorgan 1615 William Thomas of Portsmouth was concerned in a suit about 13 bales of corn. 8th of St. Michael's Term Anno 51–52 Henry III. Placitorum abbreviatio. 166 Rotuli Normanniae. Giles Thomas was Treasurer of the Duke of Brittany Nov. 22. 1483 ; John Thomas, John Duboys & John Morgan Merchants have license to go into Normandy with two ships. Sept. 28. 1417 ; Rotuli Hundredorum i. 63. Adam Thomas was a jurat of Villata de Asp'ton Co Devon Anno 3. Edward I.

William Thomas born at Bristol in 1613, chaplain to Duke of York and Preceptor to Princess Anne, afterwards Lord Bishop of Worcestor d. 1689 was of a very ancient and noble family as appears by his pedigree taken out of the Heralds office in 1688 to prove his right to the Arms of Herbert. His father was John Thomas, Linen draper of Bristol, who lived in his own house on the Bridge in that town, his grandfather was Recorder of Caermarthen, where the family had lived long time with great credit. The Bishop's son William b. 1670 was Rector of St. Nicholas in Worcestor, in 1723 published a survey of Worcestor Cathedral and other works and d. in 1728. Swansea Parish Church, St. Mary's has an East window in the decorated style in its chancel the only part of the church dates back of 1739 when the rest of the church fell down. This window is said to contain the Thomas arms.

Archaeologia Cambrensis. 2. iv. 31. Sybil dau. of Walter Vaughan Constable of Huntington Castle, Hereford and his wife Elizabeth dau. of Sir James Baskerville Knt. md. John Scudamore of Holm Lacey a Gentlemen Usher to King Henry VIII, and their grandaughter Sybil Scidamore md. Thomas ap Rice.

CHEW.

The only printed pedigree referred to, is in Abram's History of Blackburn. In the materials for a history of Henry VI. wars in France published by the Master of the Rolls mention is made of the Serjeantry of Cheux in Normandy. Chew Magna, and Chewton are villages in Somersetshire England. The only arms ascribed to Chew (of London and Bedfordshire) are: Azure, a Catherine Wheel, or, between two griffin's heads erased, argent. Crest: a griffin sejant argent gutte'e de sang; beaked, legged, and winged sable, reposing his dexter foot on a catherine wheel gules. Granted Sept. 15. 1703 The arms engraved are to be found on a seal ring used by Dr. Sam'l Chew Chief

Justice of Newcastle, Kent, & Sussex Counties Pennsylvania, at about the same date as the above grant in England.

Rotuli Hundredorum. Published by Record Commission Mabilia Chieue (? Chive) holds lands of Lord Nicholas de Segrave in Stanton, Cambridgeshire. Anno 7 Edward I.

Domestic State Papers. John Ballow and Thomas Chewe, owners of the Alexander of London, John Easter, Master, have letters of marque and commission to take pirates dated Aug. 3. 1627. John Chewe late his Majesty's post at Bewdley petitions the Council stating at his entrance into said place be paid £100. and has been at continual charge to keep men and horses to perform the service which has obliged him to sell his lands and estate. Is behind in his pay £471. 4 Shills. and is indebted. Is upward of 90 years of age, with many children and grandchildren. Prays he may receive relief or his creditors will cast him into prison. May 10. 1639

"John Chewe of Bewdley Co. Worcester. Gent. Whereas there is justly due unto me from my Soveraigne Lord & Master King Charles now King of England and his royal father of ever blessed memory King James late King of this Kingdom deceased the Sum of four hundred and fifty pounds & more for my Salary and fee behind and at this present to me unpaid for his majesty's service and his said late father King James done by me in my Post Master's place in the town of Bewdley which I now serve & hold under his Majesty.

To my loving son John Chewe £5. To my daughter Dyna wife of Thomas Berkham 40 s. To my daughter Susan wife of John Leland 40 s. To my daughter Hester wife of Edmond Duncombe 40 s. To my daughter Sarah wife of John Eldridge £5. To John Harman. To Henry Coles my servant "my white suite of apparell wt, glasse buttons which is now at Bewdley" To young Thomas Bowyer who used to walk and dress my horses. To my old servant Alice Bowyer. To my dearly beloved daughter-in-lawe Elizabeth Chew the now wife of my beloved son Samuel Chewe whom I much respect for her tender care love & goodness towards me at all times the sum of £5—for a gold ring to wear in remembrance of me. Lastly in respect of the dutiful-care and regard wch my said son Samuel

Snowden

Chewe now hath & ever hath had of me and my prosperity &c. I bequeath him the rest and residue of my goods &c. and make him Executor.

Witnesses Benjamin Wilson, William Hiett, Thomas Gardon & Thomas Dunn (11 Coventry) Dated April 9. 1636. proved 17. Jany. 1639–40.

Gentleman's Magazine. 1783. Names James Chew of Bristol, Somersetshire in a list of bankrupts; In a list of the inhabitants of Flushing Long Island in 1698. appear Richard Chew & Ffrances his wife, Rich'd, Henry, Tho, Hannah, Charley, Mary, and Elizabeth. In the Surrogates office New York are the Wills of Thomas Chew made Sept. 30. 1846 and of Robert Chew then in New York, made Nov. 20. 1860.

SNOWDEN.

Domestic State Papers. Richard Snowden, Merchant is taken prisoner by the rebels in Ireland in July. 1529. John Snowden who returned to England in 1591 which he left in 1582 was a priest, born in Worcester, a spy of Burleigh's, but would not "inform against a Catholic for religion but only for treason." "A mean fellow Dr. Robert Snowden made Bishop of Carlisle in 1616." George Snowden of Ashe, Co. Kent mentioned May. 7. 1622. Thomas Snowden has a grant of an almsroom in St. Stephen's Westminister Oct. 15. 1631. S. P. D. Luke Snowden aged 21 years having a certificate from the Minister of Gravesend embarqued in the Primrose for Virginia. July 27. 1635. Hotten's Lists. Rutland Snoden, Justice of the Peace Co. Lincoln, June 30. 1686 S. P. D. Ditto. a delinquent Apl.

22. 1648. 7th Report Hist. Mss. Commission. John Snowden signs a testimonial of Gisborough Friends' Meeting Yorkshire 3 mo. 28th 1754. Henry Snowden of Talbot Co. Maryland in his Will dated Mch. 7. 1699 proved June 20· 1699 mentions his wife Elenor, & sons William, Henry, and child his wife was now pregnant with; and daughters Rachel and Henrietta Maria. Liber H. 267 Wills at Annapolis, Md. Friends' Testimonies London 1760 contains one to Mary Snowden of Gisborough Meeting in Yorkshire d. in 6th month 1745 in the 57th year of her age. George Snowden was a Banker of Stockton on Tees Durhamshire, England in 1800.

BUCKLEY.

Domestic State Papers. Mr. Buckley a papist had a factor at Rouen in France in 1589. Sir Richard Buckley (? Bulkeley) is a justice of the peace in Cheshire suspected to be a papist in 1580. Matthew Buckley in early part of Elizabeth's reign, is accused by a servant of an intended secret departure from London. William Buckley refuses to pay money for beacons Feb. 6. 1627. Father Giles a French priest, robbed by his own servant in the house of Brandon Buckley of London Jany. 25. 1627. Richard Buckley a fellow of St. John's College Cambridge. in Oct. 1633. Thomas Buckley of Cheshire was imprisoned in 1663 for non-payment of tithes. See Besse's Sufferings of Quakers. William Buckley of Talbot Co. Maryland in his Will made Nov. 28th 1708 mentions his wife Elizabeth; children William, James, Richard, Robert Nicholas deceased & *his* wife Margaret.

LAWRENCE.

Printed Pedigrees or genealogical notices may be found in Miscellanea Gen. et. Her. I. 128. 199—212. 233. 237 New Series. I. 46. 68; Herald & Genealogist IV. 465. 529—544. VIII. 177. 188. 210; Collectanea Top. et Gen. iii. 281; Blomefield's Norfolk. V. 335; Berry's Hampshire, 248; Gentleman's Magazine. LXXXV. ii. 12. 104. 504. LXXXVII. i. 318. 518. ii. 126; Cambridgeshire Visitations ed. by Phillipps 20. Ditto of Gloucestershire. 7; Harleian Society ii. 27. 102. viii. 75; Nichols' Leicester iii. 1135, iv. 408; Hoare's Wiltshire, III. iv. 68. V. ii. 74; Chetham Society. XCV. 72. Faulkner's History of Chelsea. Burke's Peerage and Baronetage; and Landed Gentry. Cheltenham, (England) Examiner of Aug. 27 and Oct. 15. 1862. Notes & Queries has numerous brief notices for which see its indexes. Record Commission, Ducatus Lancastriae Inquisitiones I. 11. 17. 28. 32. 40, IV. 118. 163. 200. Bishop Kip's Olden Time in New York, Old Merchants of New York (see indexes) Thompson's Long Island 2d edition. Rev. John Lawrence's Genealogies of the New England family, and Thomas Lawrence's Genealogy of the Long Island family. Mss. Pedigrees may be found at the British Museum in the Mss. W. I. Registers presented by Capt. J. H. Lawrence-Archer; of Lawrence of Iver Bucks in the Heralds' Visitations 1102. Fo. 4; 1151 Fo. 2; 1193 Fo. 3; 1391 Fo. 4 b.; 1533 Fo. 161. b; Lawrence of Huntingdon: Ditto 1543. fo. 97; 1401. fo. 80; 1534 fo. 130 b. 6769 fo. 31; 6770 fo. 54; 6774 fo. 99. 6775 fo. 100; 4962 fo. 75 b. And in Rawlinson's Mss. B. LXXVII Bodleian Library, Oxford.

The principal Coats of Arms ascribed to the name are:

Laurence, of Colchester, Essex. *Ar.* a cross embattled *Gu.*

Lawrence of Iver, Bucks, and St. Ives, Hunts. *Ar.* a cross raguly *gu.* on a chief of the second a lion passant guardant. Crest: a stag's head erased *sa.* plate'e, attired *or*, ducally gorged *ar.*

Lawrence, of Hampshire: *Ar.* a cross between four cinquefoils *gu.* Crest: on a chapeau turned up *ermine*, a talbot sejant *gu.*

Lawrence, of Sandywell Park, Gloucester: *Ar.* a cross raguly *gu.* a cresent for a difference. Crest: a demi turbot.

Lawrence, of West Stocklands, Leicester: *Sa.* three lozenges *ar.* each charged with a saltire *gu.*

Lawrence, of London: Ermine, a cross raguly *gu.* a canton *sa.*

Lawrence, of Lancashire: *Ar.* a cross engrailed *gu.*, *Ar.* a cross *gu.*, and *Ar.* a cross wavy *gu.*

Lawrence, of Gloucester: *Gu.* two chevrons *Ar.* Crest: a griffin's head erased.

Lawrence, of Devon: Checquy *or* and *az.* on a bend *gu.* three escallops *ar.*

Lawrence, of no special place: A cross raguly trunked *gu.*; *Sa.* a chevron between three broken swords. *Ar.* on a chief embattled of the second, three martlets *gu.*

Lawrence, Laurence, or Lawrance, of Chelsea, Middlesex; Delaford, Chertsey and Iver, Bucks and St. Ives, Hunts: *Ar.* a cross raguly *gu.* on a chief *az.* three leopards' heads *or.* Crest: a demi-turbot or demi-dolphin erect *gu.* the tail upward.

Ditto, of Foxcote or Foxhall Co. Gloucester and Studley Royal, York: *Ar.* a cross raguly *gu.* Crest: a wolf's head *ar.* charged on the neck with a crescent *or.* Another Crest: a wolf's head *ar.* charged on the neck with a cross crosslet *gu.* Another Coat: *Ar.* a cross raguly *gu.* in the first quarter a lion passant. Crest: a wolf's head ppr. charged with a cresent *or.*

Miscellanea Genealogica et Heraldica I. 199–212 contains a collection of tabular pedigrees of Laurence, Lawrence, Lawrance and Lorance, which need a reference to the original documents for confirmation, as some at least are incorrectly described as Visitation pedigrees of a date when no visitation was made. Ditto. I. 233–237 contains a pedigree of Lawrence of Withington Co. Gloucester, drawn up April 10th, 1840, beginning in 1558.

The anonymous author of "The Normans," recently printed at London writes "William Lorenz was in Normandy 1180–1195, see 'Magno rotuli Scaccariae Normanniae.'" John, Richard and William Laurenz were in England about 1272 see " Rotuli Hundredorum."

Herald & Genealogist VIII, 212. R. Gwynne Lawrence writes "there is a continuous line of the Laurans family in France from Arnold de Lauran of Lauran near Montpellier in Languedoc A. D. 1110. In 1124 Arnault de Lauran and Pierre and Arnauld his nephews cede the Chateau to the Compte de Beziers et Carcassone. In 1236 Peter de Lauran md. Matilda dau. of Compte Amery III of Clermont-Lodere. Raymond de Lauran was living in 1309." Pere Anselme's Histoire Genealogique &c. de France notices Nicholas Laurans de Noyal who md. Aliette du Cambont in Bretagne about 1440 ; Phillippe Laurans widow of the Seigneur d' Azay le Rideau and dau. of Nicholas Laurance Seigneur de Mamez in 1499 ; Jean Laurens, Seignuur de la Noüe' in 1560 ; Jacques Laurens Seigneur de la Mothe in 1625 ; Louis Joseph de Laurens Compte d' Ampus, Capitaine de cavalerie, &c. in 1721 and several others of the name. Pedigrees of the French family may be found in More'ri's Grand dictionnaire historique etc.

The earliest of the name in Lancashire I have discovered is William Lawrence, who held in 1311 lands at Ashton, on the Ribble near Preston, in right of his wife, who was a dau. and co-heir of Heydock or Eyedock of Haydock in the same county (this seems to dispose of the crusading

Sir Robert Laurens of Ashton Hall). William Lawrence was a Burgess in Parliament 1326, and living in 1341. His son John succeeded him in his estate in 1368. His in quisition in 1399 reads: John son of William Lawrence dec. 1368 *"feoffavit Laurencium de Myerch cap . . de omnibus terris suis in Ribbleton, Ashton, Preston, Laton et Thornton." idem Johannes obiit die ante Ascensionem* 1398. William his son and heir aged 18 years, Mother, Margaret. In 1344 another William de Lawrence was seneschal, of Henry Earl of Lancaster, Steward of Blackburnshire 1351–1354. He md. Alice de Stapylton dau. of Sir Nicholas de Stapylton by Sybil dau. of Sir John de Bella Aqua, and Laderine who was dau. of Peter Brus of Skelton and Helwyse de Lancaster. William and Alice (Stapylton) Lawrence had a son and heir Sir Edmund who md. Mary ———. Had a manor *"ex dimisione"* from his grandfather, Sir Nicholas de Stapylton, and was summoned to a Parliament at Westminister in 1362 about the affairs of Ireland, as one of the heirs of Camville holding land in Ireland. As he was not again summoned, it is held that no Barony was created by this writ. His heir, apparently, was Sir Robert Lawrence, of Ashton Hall, Escheator of Lancashire in 1403, Sheriff of Lancashire 1407 and 1420 proved his arms 1419, 1427, 1429, obiit 18th, Henry VI. (1440)

According to Harleian Ms. No. 6, 159, a copy of the Visitation of Lancashire in 1567 with additional pedigrees, of which the following is one: He was the son of Edmund Lawrence and had brothers James and William, who both d. s. p.

The best supported version of this pedigree as revised by R. Gwynne Lawrence with corrections from my own researches is as follows:

Sir Robert Lawrence, who may have been Robert Lawrence, Esq., who, with two men at arms and six foot archers, was of the retinue of King Henry V, in 1417 (see Nicholas'

Agincourt, page 381); possibly md. Margaret Holden, of Lancashire. He had issue:

   i. Robert b. in 1400, of whom presently.

  ii. Edmund, who had issue: Thomas d. s. p.; Robert; John, father of John; Nicholas and James both d. s. p.

 iii. Thomas. (q. v.)

Robert, the eldest son, md. Margaret, dau. of John Lawson or Lawrence of Rixton or Raxton, and d. 1450, leaving issue: I. Sir James, Knt. of Ashton, aged 22 at his father's inquisition d. 1490, md. 1st, Cecilia Botiler; and 2d., Eleonora, dau. of Lord Welles and widow of Lord Hoo and Hastings, (Lord Hoo d. 1455,) by whom he had no issue; by his first wife he had: Sir Thomas, K. B , 1501, md. ――――, and d. before 1513, having had an only son John d. s. p. abroad before his father; and John md. ―――― and d. s. p. at Flodden in 1513, being the last male of the main line. II. Robert, killed at Bosworth in 1485, leaving issue: only daughters (who were co heiresses of their cousin John Lawrence of Ashton) Agnes md. ―――― Skillicorne; Margaret md. ―――― Rigmayden; Elizabeth md. ―――― Butler of Rawcliffe; and Alice md. ―――― Clyfton.

Thomas third son of Sir Robert Lawrence of Ashton Hall md. Mabilla dau. and heiress of John Redmayne of Yeland Redmayne and had issue: Edmund of whom presently; John; William; Robert; Richard; James all d. s. p.; and Elizabeth md. John Nausier and had issue: Agnes md. William Preston.

Edmund the eldest son of Thomas and Mabilla (Redmayne) Lawrence had issue at his death 6th Henry VIII: Lancelot. Lancelot Lawrence was heir male of the family and d. 26th Henry VIII leaving issue: Thomas; and Sir Oliver Knighted at the Battle of Musselburg in 1547 d. s. p. Thomas the eldest son d. 35th Henry VIII leaving an only son and heir Robert who d. in the second year of the reign of Philip and Mary possessed of Lands at Yeland

Redmain, Dylake, Heysham, Myddleton, Bolton, Warton, Skirton Hutton, Flokborow, and Sylverdale in Lancashire. He left an only dau. Anne aged 10 at her father's inquisition who was the sole heiress of the family and md. Walter third son of Sir John Sydenham of Brampton, Co. Somerset. See R. G. Lawrence's Article in the Herald & Genealogist VIII. 212 and authorities there referred to, most of which I have verified; also Record Publications, especially Ducatus Lancastriae I. 11. 28. 32. 40. &c. and Parliamentary Writs. I. 3d. 1084.

Robertus Laurence, Miles, d. 18th Henry VI. possessed of Bantheswerth and Dilacre Manors and Noteland *"terra et tenement."* Westmoreland. (See Duc. Lancastriae. IV. 200.)

Record Commission Publications. Rotuli Hundredorum. I. 87. Henry Laurence was a Jurat in the Hundred of Wynkelegh Co. Devon, Anno tertio Edwardi Primi. (1299) Ditto. I. 53. Gilbert Laurence paid XII Shillings to the sub-bailiff of the Hundred of Flemedich, Co. Cambridge. Anno quarto Edwardi Primi. (1300) Ditto. II. under the seventh year of Edward's reign A. D. 1303 we find pp. 363. 392. Ric's Laurence holds land by succession from Isabella his mother, to whom it was given at her marriage by Robert Seman her father. Richard Laurence had planted trees and made a bridge over the ditch or moat of Canterbury "for going out of his *averiis et pecoribus* to his pasture of Grenecroft." page 465. Robert Heved holds 3 acres in Northstowe, Co. Cambridge of Richard Laurence. 366. Richard Laurence son of Richard holds *"in feodo"* a capital messuage 4 Shills. Value of the Prior and Convent of Ely. 373. Land is bought of Rico son of Rici Laurence. Rich. Laurent holds a house near the *"Cur' Sce. Radegund."* 370-1-3. Agnes de Berton holds an acre in Canterbury given her by her son Henry de Berton which he had *"de dono Rici Laurence in libo maritagio"* with Cecilia his wife, dau. of Richard Laurence and grandaughter of Wade.

Henry & Cecilia de Berton hold land in the Parish of St. Benedict by gift of Ric. Laurence and Sabine his wife who had brothers John and Rici Ategate. Also land in St. Botolph's Parish is given by R. L. which came to him in marriage by gift of Rici Ategate. Placitorum Abbreviatio. 299. Simonis Laurenz, a clerk is delivered from prison (where he had been put on account of felony.) by order of the Papal administrators of the Archdiocese of Canterbury, St. Michael's Term 1330.

Archaeologia Cambrensis 4th. I. 49. Thomas Lawrence was receiver of Huntington Manor, Hereford in 1413. Rotuli Normanniae 66. Petrus Laurence was perpetual chaplain of St. Peters de Cadorno in Normandy Sept. 7. 1417.

Coll. Top. et. Genealogica IV. 220. Walto Le Laurence de Stylton, Hunts. signs a .charter Oct. 3. Anno Edward III "a conquestu 4th." IV. 208. John Lawrence Parson of Stavely Co. Derby, May 7. 1575. V. 86. Georgius Laurentius of London a Pilgrim to Rome Aug. 28. 1587. V. 390. Sepulchral inscription of John Laurans existed in the Church of the Grey Friars, London temp. Henry VIII. Hutchin's Dorset part IV. gives some account of the Crick or Creech Grange in Steple Parish, Family descended from Sir Oliver Lawrence Knt. who bought the Grange in 1540, called Grandson of Sir Robert Law-rence of Lancashire. It is to be noted there were Martyn, and Christopher Lawrence in that Parish in 1524 (See Herald and Gen. II. 140). The arms · in Steple Church are Lawrence and Washington quarterly with a crescent for difference. These appear in the Lancashire Visitation of 1567 Harleian Ms. 891, without the crescent.

ARMS OF

LAWRENCE AND WASHINGTON.

123

A list printed in 1590 includes John Lawrence burned at Colchester, Mch. 29. 1555, and Henry Lawrence burned at Canterbury in Aug. 1555, See Notes & Queries, Aug. 17. 1878.

Rolls Publications. Domestic State Papers. Antony Laurence Custom House Deputy at Parton Creek, Cumberland Apl. 28. 1566. Jenkyn Lawrence a Commissioner for the Musters in Dorset in 1570. Lady Lawrence of Hampshire "a godly woman and great housekeeper at whose house the Queen (Elizabeth) was last Summer" mentioned in a letter Jan. 21. 1570. John Laurens writes from Rouen to William Allambrigge and his sister Joan Laurens at Cerne Mch. 13. 1585. John Lawrence holds Sywardsly pasture and wood in Woodwalton and Denton, Co. Northampton June 17. 1602 and traces descent of the land from time of Edward II. Ambrose Lawrence was administrator of Andrew Linge July 4. 1626. John Lawrence one of his Majesty's Musicians July 11. 1626. William Lawrence, keeper of the great instores at Chatham Jany. 7. 1627. William Phipps clerk has a suit against Lady Elizabeth Lawrence, Widow, Jany. 27. 1630. William Lawrence a petitioner to the Admiralty Jany. 31. 1631. Charles Lawrence and R. Wright have a grant of the office of Customer at Poole, Co. Dorset Oct. 24. 1631. Jacobus Laurentius President of the Classis of Amsterdam Apl. 26. 1633. John Lawrence owner of Parsonage house of Marks Tey, Essex, June 18. 1635. Sir John Lawrence of Chelsea, Middlesex signs a petition about Ship money in March. 1636. Robert Lawrence and Hugh Hill lessees of Braybrooke Manor. May. 26. 1636. Fitzwilliam Lawrence a registrar of the Diocese of Hereford, July 8. 1637. Sir John Lawrence and Sir Robert Poyntz had married sisters and co-heirs before 1636. Thomas Lawrence Alderman of Colchester May, 5. 1637. Simon Lawrence receiver of Lord Clare's London rents. June 26. 1669. Edward Lawrence in a commission at Dorchester Sept. 24. 1638. Funeral certificate of Sir John Lawrence of Chelsea, and Delaford and Iver, Co. Bucks who md. Grissel dau. and

IN CRUCE SALUS.

Lawrence.

co-heir of Jervas Gibbons of Benenden, Kent, and left issue at his death this day John, Robert. Henry, Anne, Frances, Grissel, Nov. 12. 1638. John Lawrence is a Parliamentary Captain of Horse in Norfolk Feby. 27. 1650. Henry Lawrence was paid £215.17.2d. for freight of the Elizabeth of London with provisions to the Army in Ireland Oct. 1. 1651. Col. Lawrence was of the Army in Ireland. Nov. 11. 1652. Major Richard Lawrence is to be sent to the Grand Seignior from the Council of State Mch. 9. 1653. Is Agent of the Levant Company at Constantinople June 19. 1654. Is to be paid $4000 and his expenses for his year there Sept. 25. 1654. William Lawrence is one of the Civil Commissioners for Justice in Oct. 1653. Henry Lawrence (the Lord President) added to the Council of State July 14. 1653. The President's first recorded ancestor was an Edmund Lawrence called 4th son of Sir Robert Lawrence of Ashton Hall (This seems merely an attempt to make a connexion with the Lancashire family as there is no evidence offered to substantiate the claim) Edmund had issue: Richard who had a son John; and John Lawrence de Wurdeboys who was Abbot of Ramsey Abbey in Huntingdonshire from 1507; in 1539 he was not only very forward in procuring his own Abbey to be surrendered to the King but influenced others to submit, for which service he obtained according to Dugdale the large pension of £266.13.6d. per annum. In his will dated in 1541 and proved in Nov. 1542 (registro Spert) he makes considerable bequests to the Churches of St. Ives, Ramsey and Burwell, leaves £10. among twenty paupers and his silver plate &c. to his cousin William Lawrence. He desires to be buried in St. Mary's Burwell and appoints William Lawrence of St. Ives one of his executors. John son of Richard and nephew of the Lord Abbot, styled in all evidences "generosus", d. in 1538, leaving by his will (registro Dingley) besides considerable donations to the church, two of his best mares to my Lord of Ramsey for supervising his will. He had issue: Emma md. Gabriel 3d. son of Richard Throckmorton of Higham Ferrers, Sen-

eschal of the Duchy of Lancaster, Agnes md. Gilbert Smyth
of Fenton, and William who settled at St. Ives, was High
Sheriff of Cambridge and Hunts at the death of Queen Mary,
and was buried at St. Ives Dec. 20. 1572. By his will (registro Peter) he bequeathes to his son Henry his armour,
the plate he inherited from his uncle the Abbot of Ramsey,
and "the iron chest in the Library containing papers which
had been particularly mentioned in the will of his father."
He md. 1st. Frances Houston, and had by her his heir Henry
of whom presently, and William; (ancestor of the Lawrences
of Chichester and Aldingbourne) md. 2d. Margaret dau. of
Edward Kaye of Woodson in Yorkshire and had further
issue: Robert d. in 1597 (ancestor of the Lawrences of Norfolk) Henry the eldest son md. Elizabeth dau. of John
Hagar of Bourne Castle Cambridgeshire and was buried at
St. Ives Feby. 25. 1580-1, having had a son and heir John,
Knighted by James I. in 1603 at Windsor, md. Elizabeth
sole dau. and heir of Ralph Waller of Beaconsfield, who
after his death md. 2d. Robert Bathurst, Sheriff of Gloucestershire. Sir John Lawrence was buried at St. Ives Feby.
10. 1604. In his will (made Jan. 10. proved Feb. 9. 1604
Registro Hayes) he mentions his two sons Henry and John.
The former was then aged 3 years 2 months and 4 days.
(Cole's Escheats. Harl. Ms. 760) He entered Emanuel Coll.
Cambridge in 1622 as a fellow commoner, B. A. 1623, M. A.
1627. In 1641 was in Parliament as a Knight of the Shire
for Westmoreland. From a preface to a work of his printed
in 1646 it appears that he was abroad at the begining of the
Civil War, "the warre found me abroad not sent me thither,
and I have beene onely wary without a just and warrantable
reason to ingage my selfe in that condition from which a
a providence seem'd to rescue mee." He seems to have
found such reason shortly thereafter as he appears as a
member of Parliament for Hertfordshire in 1653 and July
14. of that year is added to the Council of State by Cromwell, July 27. is on the Committee of Foreign Affairs
was present at 17 Sittings of the Council in Nov. and Dec.

1653, and at 164 in 1654 being the only member present at all the sittings. Dec. 19. 1653 Cromwell appointed him Lord President of the Council for one month from date. Jan. 16. 1653-4 there was an order by the Protector that Hen. Lawrence be continued President of the Council until further order Feby. 9. 1654 we find him paid £300 apparently his salary. Notices of his action as Lord President may be found in Domestic State Papers for 1653-4. He was elected M. P. for Colchester and Carnarvonshire in 1656 and chose to sit for the latter Shire. In Dec. 1657 he was gazetted a Lord of the Other House, Cromwell's attempt at a life peerage. As Lord President he took the responsibility of proclaiming Richard Cromwell as his father's successor, but on the Restoration of Charles II was allowed to return to private life. He opposed the execution of Charles I. and there is in Thurloe's State Papers a letter to him from the Queen of Bohemia recommending Lord Craven to his good graces and saying she knew he had only accepted office, in order to render services to those who needed them. He published at Amsterdam in 1646 "Militia Spiritualis, a treatise of our Communion and Warre with Angels"; in the same year an annonymous treatise "on Baptism"; in 1649 "A Vindication of the Scriptures," and in 1652 "Gospel Ordinances." The author has a copy of the 3d edition of the first treatise "on Angels," formerly in the possession of the Woollaston-White family, heirs of the Presidents grandson Sir Edward Lawrence Bart. Afterwards in that of Capt. J. H. Lawrence-Archer who has made some Mss. memoranda relating to the Lawrence Genealogy of which I have made use in the above sketch of the Lord President's ancestry, in connexion with the Memoir written by Sir James Lawrence, Knight of Malta, and the English State Papers. Capt. Archer also had a photograph made of the unique drawing in the Queen's copy of Clarendon's Rebellion, at Windsor Castle, from which the engraved portrait of the President was facsimiled. He is called Sir Henry Lawrence tho' I have seen no record

of his ever having been Knighted. He md. Amy dau. of
Sir Edward Peyton Bart. of Iselham in Cambridgeshire and
d. Aug. 8. 1664 intestate. Capt. Archer says the records of
the Probate Court show his widow was administratrix; but
Sir James Lawrence states that his son Henry administered
the estate. According to his gravestone (visible in 1802) in
the Chapel at St. Margaret's Als Thele in Hertfordshire the
President had issue seven sons and six daughters. Henry
M. P. for Carnarvonshire in 1656 d. in 1679 leaving issue:
Henry d. u., and Edward created a Baronet with remainder
to his sisters son and d. May. 2. 1749; Edward M. P. for
Pembrokeshire in 1656 and d. in 1657; John, emigrated to
Jamaica; William and Martha naturalized as born abroad
Nov. 27. 1656, the latter md. Richard Earl of Barrymore;
Elizabeth d. in Feb. 1662 aged 30; Theodosia d. Sept. 2.
1664 aged 20; Henrietta d. Sept. 30. 1664 aged 13; the others
I have not been able to trace. John Milton is said to have
assisted in the composition of the treatise on Angels, and he
addressed the President's son Henry in the Sonnet beginning
"Lawrence of virtuous father virtuous son."

John Lawrence brother of the Lord President d. in 1670
leaving an only son Dr. Thomas Lawrence Physician to five
crowned heads. He d. in 1714 leaving a numerous issue; of
whom the eldest a Captain in the Navy was father of Thomas
Lawrence President of the College of Physicians and grandfather of Sir Soulden Lawrence. Of this family were the
Lawrences of Hackfall, and Studley Royal with Fountain's
Abbey Yorkshire.

The Irish family of the name whose members have in
the last century distinguished themselves in India and the
East, descends from an unknown stock, but has always
claimed to have the same ancestry, and Maj. Gen. Stringer
Lawrence, Sir Henry Lawrence, and Lord Lawrence, the
Viceroy of India, are scions of which any family might be
proud.

Milner's Winchester Notices Mayors of the Town of the
name, W. Lawrence 1525; Wm. Lawrence 1532, 1553, 1574;

ST. ALBANS, HERTFORDSHIRE.

Gilbert Lawrence 1545   In the Library of St Mary's College
Winchester is an Explanation of the Epistles of St. Paul by
James Lawrence 4°. Amsterdam 1642.   Peter Lawrence exe-
cutes deeds for land at Birdbroke or Badbrooke Co. Essex in
1687 and 1689.   Rev. H. J. B. Nicholson Rector of Great
St. Albans England writes Major J. H. Lawrence-Archer
that the Parish Records of one of the Parishes were
burned with the Rectory in 1745 there are however two
others St. Michael and St. Peter.   John Lawrence was Mayor
1567 and 1575.   Of the Chief Burgesses were John Lawrence 1553 Barnaby 1574 and Thomas 1622.

Mr. G. D. Scull writes to me from England Mch. 14, 1878
"With the greatest inducement being an old ardent and
experienced Genealogist I have sought for proof that my
ancestor (William Lawrence of Flushing) was related to
the Cromwells and Henry Lawrence his Lord President.
This I have utterly failed to do, & I now believe no proof
exists to justify such claims."   From the authorities to
which Mr. Scull refers me in the latter part of his letter, I
am disposed to question his "experience" as a Genealogist.
They are merely such printed Articles on the pedigree, as
the veriest tyro should have examined before beginning his
investigations.   At the same time I must agree with him
that there is no proof offered to show the connexion, while I
would hesitate to say there is none extant.   Mr. Scull has
since the date of his letter discovered a record of the marriage
of William Lawrence and Joan Brooke on the Register of
St. Stephen's Church just outside of St. Albans dated Feby.
16. 1617–18.   From the appropriateness of the wife's Christian name, and the date of the marriage, to the name of the
mother and ages of the children who emigrated from St.
Albans in the "Planter" in 1635 I have no reasonable doubt
they were the ancestors of the American family, but nothing
has been learned as to the pedigree of this William Lawrence
of St. Albans.   That he was of Gentle birth may be presumed
from the use of a Seal of Arms by his son Thomas Lawrence

of Newtown in 1699. The seal attached to the original will (proved Mch. 28. 1698-9. Recorded in Liber 5, page 336.) at the Surrogate's office, New York City, is a small one of red wax, not a good impression, but certainly not the arms of Lawrence of Ashton. The Crest appears to be a wolf's head, charged in the neck with a very distinct crescent, the shield apparently has three figures, lions rampant or other animals it is impossible to say. Undoubtedly there is no cross. The crest agrees with that of Lawrence of Foxhall, Gloucester, the arms with no recorded coat.

Calendar New York Hist. Mss. 1630-1664 Boston Sept. 15. 1658 Letter of Gov. Endicott and Comm'rs. of United New England Colonies in favour of John Lawrence.

A copy of the long and elaborate Will of John Lawrence Senr. (the Emigrant) "Susanno de Widdowe" executrix, may be found in the Surrogate's office, New York. Liber 5 folio 346. Proved May, 15. 1699. The clerk reported Nov. 7, 1881 that there are no original wills of that year in the office.

An inventory of the estate of William Lawrence (the Emigrant) may be found in Liber 2. folios 212 to 228. This document dated April 9. 1680 states that he died intestate, and values his entire estate £4432.1s.10½d.

Other Lawrence Wills in the Surrogate's office New York City. with year of probate and, in parenthesis, the Liber and folio.

Abraham R. 1866 (164. 27) Adam, 1780, (34. 97 & 39. 428) Alexander 1853. (105. 425) Ann, 1821 (56. 538) Augustus, 1794 (41. 285) Augustine H. 1828 (62. 262) Caleb, 1799 (43.110) Catherine, 1807. (47. 97). 1834. (73. 84) Daniel, 1757 (20. 322) Deborah, 1743 (15. 47.) 1812, (50. 118) Edward, 1832 (69. 60) Edward B. 1863, (148. 452) Edward N. 1840 (81. 113) Eleanor, 1837 (76. 130) Elizabeth, 1851 (101. 409) Jacob, 1771 (28. 23) Jacobus, 1780 (34. 60) John of Flushing on Nassau Island, dated, Sept. 29, 1712 mentions his wife Elizabeth and

PER FIDEM ET CONSTANTIAM

Schieffelin

children, William, Richard, Benjamin, Charity, Sarah. Elizabeth Fford and Mary Briggs. Proved Feb. 21. 1714 (8. 332) John, 1764 (24. 481) 1765 (25. 108) 1767, (26. 134) 1794 (41. 338) Jonathan, 1767 (25. 448) Joseph of Flushing Yeoman, mentions his wife, his sons Richard and John and daughters Elizabeth Bowne, Sarah Lawrence, Hannah Molynex, and Abigil Fforbes, dated Dec. 8. 1754, proved Apl. 18. 1759 (22.7) Mary, 1763, (23.544) 1784 (37. 230) Norris 1790 (40. 430) Obadiah 1733 (11. 475) Patience 1773 (28.365) Richard of New York Mariner, date Sept. 16. 1706, children Charity and Richard who is not 4 months old, Father in law, Thomas Clarke, and Brother in law William Glencross. proof 1711 (8. 69) Richard 1781. (34. 416) 1784 (36. 447) 1784 (37. 133) Samuel, 1760, (22. 148) Sarah, 1740 (13. 361) Silas, 1782 (34. 523) Stephen, 1781 (34. 344) Thomas Feb. 12. 1703 (7. 134 no seal of arms) 1752 (18. 202) 1784 (36. 405) Thomas S. 1763 (23. 570) William of Flushing, wife Deborah, children Elizabeth, Joshua, Caleb, Stephen, Obediah, Daniel, Samuel and Adam. Proof July 28. 1719 (9. 152) William of Newtown, Yeoman, wife Elizabeth, sons, William, Samuel, John. dated Dec. 3. 1731 Proved Feb. 11. 1731-2. (11. 218) William, 1758 (21. 24) 1772 (28. 288)

In the Herald and Genealogist IV. 465 is a tabular pedigree of Lawrence of Philadelphia descended from Thomas Lawrence said to have been born at St. Albans, England, in 1666 emigrated to New England md. Catherine Lewis May 10. 1687 and d. in 1739. Latest date in pedigree 1857. From Monumental Inscriptions in the British West Indies by Capt. J. H. Lawrence–Archer, London 4°. 1875, with additions from the author's Mss. Tombstone of (Major) John Lawrence. d. t. l. Jany. 7. 1718-19 in 46th year of his age. He was a buccaneering commander under Sir Henry Morgan. Rev. Richard Brisset Lawrence d. Oct. 13 1831 aged 31 years 3 mos. Hon. Col. James Lawrence of Fairfield, Jamaica buried June 15. 1756 in 47 year of his age. Note. John supposed son of President Henry Lawrence (q. v.) Emigrated

to Barbadoes and returned to Jamaica (will May 10. 1690)
md. 1675 Jane (Collins) Dunn and had 3 sons and 6 daughters, the third son was Col. James, above mentioned, who
md. Mary dau. of Col. Richard James and had an eldest
son Richard James who md. Mary 4th dau. of Thomas Hall
of Kirkpatrick, and d. Nov. 8. 1830 having had 5 sons:
Sir James, Knight of Malta, author of "the Nobility of
the British Gentry" &c.; George; Charles; Henry; and
Frederick Augustus. John eldest son of the Emigrant
John Lawrence md. Susannah Petgrave and d. in 1725.
Their dau. Susanna md. Lawrence Lawrence (Will 1743)
and had Rachel md. Lieut. Col. Harry Gordon (Will
1787). Their dau. Ann. md. Alexander Edgar, of some
place in Lanark (Will 1820) and had Mary md. J. H. Archer
(Will 1840) whose son was Capt. J. H. Lawrence-Archer.
(See also Roby's History of the Parish of St. James Jamaica
part. 3d.)

Hotten's Original lists of Emigrants &c. New York 1874 ;
Notices that Henry Lawrence owned 10 acres of land and 6
negroes in St. James' Parish, Barbadoes, Dec. 20. 1629.

Coll. Top. et. Gen. ii. 281. Sir John Lawrence of Chelsea, and Deláford in Iver, Bucks, Knighted at Royston Jan.
26. 1609–10 created a Baronet Oct 9. 1628 Arms, Az. a cross
raguly gu. on a chief az. 3 Leopard's heads or, this chief &c.
evidently taken from the arms of the Goldsmith's Company.
He was son and heir of Thomas Lawrence of London as usual
said to descend from Lawrence of Lancashire who d. Oct. 28.
1594. Sir John md. Grissell dau. and co-heir of Gervase
Gibbon of Benenden in Kent and d. Nov. 13. 1638 aged 50.
He had 7 sons and 4 dau. His grandson the 3d Baronet
was Sir Thomas Lawrence who was Secretary of the Colony
of Maryland. According to Hotten's Lists was so Sept. 5. 1691.
Sept. 20. 1698 Letters appointing Sir Thos. Lawrence Bart.
revoked and Thomas Lawrence Esquire appointed during
pleasure July 11. 1701 appointed during pleasure as "Sir
Thomas Lawrence Bart. He is said to have been buried at
Chelsea Apl. 25. 1714. He md. Anne dau. of Mrs. E. English

who was buried at Chelsea in 1710 and had issue: Anne baptized there May. 4. 1675 and John baptized there Nov. 5. 1676. Anne Lady Lawrence was buried at Chelsea Nov. 2. 1723. John heir apparent of Sir Thomas and Anne his wife sold an estate at Chelsea Mch. 26. 1706. his wife Elizabeth was buried there Aug. 7. 1701.

Sheafe and Satterthwaite.

Sampson son of Edmund Sheafe b. at Boston in 1650 md. Mehitable dau. of Jacob Sheafe of Boston and d. in 1724, leaving a son Sampson b. in 1681 md. Sarah dau. of Col. Theodore Walton and d. in 1772, leaving a son Jacob b. in 1715 md. in 1740 Hannah dau. of Col. Shadrach Seavy and d. in —— leaving a son James b. Nov. 17. 1755 was of Portsmouth, New Hampshire, and md. July 13th, 1800, as his 2d wife Sarah dau. of John Fisher and Ann dau. of Hon. Mark Hanking Wentworth, and d. Dec. 5. 1829 ; his wife d. Feb. 7. 1863 aged 88 years having had issue :

i. Ann Fisher, of whom presently.

ii. Louisa b. in 1803, md. Alfred W. Haven and d. in 1828 leaving issue: Louisa Sheafe md. Mark Freeman.

iii. Elizabeth Wentworth d. u. in 1814.

iv. John Fisher md. Mary dau. of Robert Lennox of New York.

v. George b. in 1825 d. u. in 1825.

vi. James Edward b. in 1810, d. at St. Augustine, Florida in 1830.

Ann Fisher eldest dau. of Hon James and Sarah (Fisher) Sheafe b. in 1801 md. in 1837, Thomas Wilkinson son of Thomas Wilkinson and (Catherine Bache) Satterthwaite descended from Thos. Wilkinson Satterthwaite, of London, England and had surviving issue death in 1815 :

i.   Elizabeth Wentworth b. in 1839 md. in 1863 John S. Condit who d. in 1869 leaving issue: Wentworth b. in 1865; Elsie b. in 1867; and John Paul b. in 1869.

ii. James Sheafe b. in 1840 md. Dec. 6. 1865 Jane Lawrence dau. of Phineas Henry and Julia (Lawrence) Buckley, and has issue: Katherine Bache b. Nov. 6. 1866; Julia Lawrence b. July 1. 1867; Annie Fisher b. June 6. 1870; James Sheafe, Jr. b. Jany. 8. 1873; and Thomas Wilkinson b. Dec. 25. 1876.

iii. Sarah Fisher md. in 1879 Rev. William R. Nairn now Rector of Grace Church, Franklin, New Jersey, and has issue: Archibald Robinson b. in 1880; and Louisa Fisher b. in 1881.

iv. Dr. Thomas Edward b. in 1844.

v.   John Fisher b. in 1845.

RAWLE. Mary Anna youngest dau. of Edward and Elizabeth (Chew) Tilghman md. William Rawle and had issue:

i.   William Henry md. 1st Mary, dau. of Hon. John Cadwalader and had issue: Mary md. Frederick Rhinelander Jones, and Edith; md. 2d, Emily, dau. of Gen. Thomas Cadwalader.

ii. Elizabeth Tilghman md. Charles Wallace Brooke of Philadelphia and had issue: Elizabeth Tilghman; William Rawle, changed his name to William Brooke Rawle and md. Elizabeth Norris Pepper; Charlotte; and Charles Wallace d. y.

134

ADDENDA.

Addressed "For Mother Thomas at heer hous on ye Poynt."

In ye name of God Amen X I Phillip Thomas of ye County of
Annarundell In ye provence of Maryland being weake' in body but of
sound & perfect memory & being made sensible of ye unccertainty of
this mortall Life & ye sertainty of Deat have Thought covenant to will
& bequeath of my worldly Istate as follocth in this my last will &
testament   Irs. I Bequeath my soull to my Redeemer & my Body
to the dust from whence it came   Irs. I will & bequeath unto my
two Sonns Philip Thomas And Sam¹¹ Thomas five hundred acrs of land
lying att ye Clefts in Calvert County in ye foresaid Province of Maryland caled Beakely & ye same to bee equallie divided betwene them
or to bee sold by them as my said suns shall think fitt   Irs. I
will & bequeath unto my beloved & faithful wife Sarah Thomas all
ye poynt of Land called fullers-poynt being one hundred & twenty
acars & lying in The¦ County of Annarundell aforesaid to be disposed
of or Imployed or sold for ye only use of & behoofe of my wife as shee
shall think good   Irs. I give & bequeath unto my said wife five
hundred acars of Land called ye playns lying in puttapsco River in
ye County of Baltemore in ye province of Maryland to be disposed
Imployed for ye only (*profit*): (*or*) yous of my sd wife ass shee shall
think good during her naturall life & after to bee delivered to my sun
Sam¹¹ as his posesion   Irs. I give & bequeath unto my said wife,
all my personall Estate, both moveable & immoveable, viz: goods mar-
chandise plate money sarvants chattles Eaither In this province or Else
whear except what before two my two suns & what after shall bee
mentioned or disposed of by me   Irs I give & bequeath unto my
sun Sam¹¹ Thomas four Cowes or heaifers to bee delivered to him forth
withafter my decese & one feather Bead   Irs. I give and bequeath
unto my Dafter Martha Thomas four Cows or heaifers to be delivered
unto hoer forth with after my desccase & one feather bead.   Irs. I
give & bequeath unto my grand Child Mary the Dafter of John Mears

five Eues to be delivered to the Sd John Mears forth with after my desease to be kept by him for ye yous of ye said Mary   Ips. I give & bequeath unto my two grandchildren Phillip and Elizabeth ye sun & Dafter of Wm Coale nine eues & one Rame to be delivered unto ye sd Wm Coale forth with after my Deseas for ye yous of ye sd Phillip & Elizabeth   Ips. I give & bequeath unto my wife afore sd ye Rent Rents & Revenues of two houses y^t I have in Bristol During her naturall Life and after to bee sould and the produce thear of to bee equally divided between my five Children viz Phillip Sam^{ll} Sarah Elizabeth and Martha   Ips. I give & bequeath unto ye Coman stock for the Relefe of pore frends Caled quakers four hundred pounds of tobacco to bee payd forth with after my deseas   Ips. I will & declare my trew & loveing wife Sarah Thomas afore sd to bee my (*whle*) & sole Executrix of this my Last will & testament.   Ips. I will & desieir y^t if itt shuld soe hapen y^t aney difference or contravarsey shuld arise after my desease betwene aney of my children and my wife concarning ye primises aforesd y^t then itt bee broght Before & a Judged of by ye body of frends Comonly Called quakers & what theay shall agree upon in that behalfe is by mee Rattefied & a Lowed of to stand in Law to all Intents & porposes   Ips. I will & declare this to bee my last will & testament hereby Disanuling & making voyd all other wills or Testements by me formerly made In withness whearof I have here unto sett my hand & seal Dated this ninth day of ye seventh month Called September Anno
                    1674

Singed Sealed & Delivered   PHILLIP THOMAS.
     in ye prs^t of us
John Ricke   Probated
Marmueduke Noble   July 10th 1675

Arms of the Skipwith Family.

OF PRESTWOULD, LEICESTERSHIRE.

Borne by SIR PEYTON D'ESTOTEVILLE, the Tenth Baronet, in 1882: Descended from SIR HENRY SKIPWITH, created Baronet Dec. 20th, 1622, and whose great grand-daughter, CASSANDRA, daughter of SIR GRAY, the Third Baronet, married PHILIP COALE at Friends' Meeting House, West River, Ann Arundel County, Maryland, on 6th April, 1697.

A Regester* of the Birthes and Burialls of ffriends and their Children
that belongs to the men and weomens meeting at west River
In Ann Arundell County In the Province of Maryland; 1674;

Day. Month. Year.

6.	9.	1658.	Talbott, Edward s. of Rich and Eliz: of Annarun-dell County "month called novefember "
21.	7.	1655.	Coale, Wm. Juni: s. of Wm. and Ester of annarun-dell County
15.	1.	1660-1.	Hooker, Joanna d. of Thomas and Joan, of annarun-dell County
7.	8.	1659	Galloway, Samuel s. of Richard and Hannah of ann-arundell County
13.	5.	1662.	Hooker, Thomas Juni: s. of Thomas and Joan.
28.	11.	1663	Galloway, Richard s. of Richard and Hannah.
12.	6.	1665	Hooker, Jacob s. of Tho; and Joan.
19.	11.	1667	Hooker, Damaris d. of Tho: and Joan.
20.	8.	1667	Coale, Wm. s. of Wm. and Hannah.
7.	2.	1668	Gilles, Elizabeth d. of John and Mary.

10.	1.	1667	Giles, Nathaniel s. of John and Mary.

7.	11.	1670.	Gilles, John Juni: s. of Jno. and Mary.
26.	6.	1668	Richardson, Wm. Juni: s. of Wm. & Eliz:
18.	1.	1670	" Daniell s. " " " " .
15.	11.	1670	Hooker, Benja. s. of Tho: and Joan.
13.	3.	1671	Richardson, Joseph s. of Wm. & Eliz:
18.	9.	1670	Skipw th, Elizabeth d. of Geo & Eliz:
30.	6.	1671	Coale, Elizabeth d. of Wm. and Eliz:
6.	7.	1673	" Phillip s. " " " " :
11.	4.	1673	Gilles, Jacob s. of Jno: & Mary.

*This "Regester" is from a small folio volume in the possession of the Yearly Meeting of Friends, on Lombard Street, Baltimore, and is the earliest Record book of the Society in Maryland. The first few leaves have ragged edges, otherwise it is perfect, I have copied the names and dates exactly, giving in addition any peculiar expression or spelling of the original. The entries are in various handwritings, and usually separated by a line or dash. I have distinguished the pages by a line under the last entry of each page. The first entry was upon the fly leaf opposite the be-ginning of the Register. I have used the following abbreviations: d.-daughter; d. h. n. l.-departed his (or her) natural life; d i. n. l.-departed is natural life; d. t. b.-departed the body; d. t. l.-departed this life; d. t. n. l.-departed this natural life; s.-son.

Day.	Month.	Year.	
4.	5.	1675	Richardson, Sophia Eliz: d. of Wm. & Eliz:
31.	6.		Hooker, Mary Ann d. of Th & Joan.
9.	2.	1676	Coale, Samuell s. of Wm. & Eliz:
20.	9.	1669.	Coale, Hannah wife of Wm., d. t. b.
12.	12.	1676	Hooker, Joan wife of Tho: d. t. b. "mo. caled ffeb."
23.	3.	167-.	Billingsly, Rebecka d. of ffrancis and Sussanna.
2.	7.	1678	Mary Ann dau. of Joan Hooker, "Departed the body it being upon a second Day of the weeke in the forenoone.
2.	7.	1678	Sophia Eliz: d. of Wm. & Eliz: Richardson "Departed the body it being upon a second Day of the weeke."
29.	8.	1678	Skipw th, Cassandra d. of Geo: & Eliz:
3.	2.	1678.	Richardson, Joseph s. of Wm. and Eliz:
1.	11.	1679-80	Hillen, Johannes s. of Johannes and Joanna.
4.	6.	16—	Giles, Artridg d. of John & Mary.
7.	4.	——	Skw th, George s. of Geo
27 ?	5.	1680	Richardson, Sapphira and Elizabeth Dauthers of Wm. and Eliz: "Sapbira Being ye first Boarn"
26.	12.	1681-2	Hillen, Deborah d. of Johannes & Joanna it being on the first Day of the weeke.
6.	12.	1680.	Talbott, Richard s. of Edw d & Eliz:
26.	9.	1681.	Talbott, Richard s. of Edw d & Eliz: dec.
14.	5.†	168-	Hillen, John dec. (month called January)
3.	10.	1682	Talbott, Edward of Edward and Elizabeth, furst day of ye weeke about ye Seckand our of ye Day.
24.	10.	-682	Arnelld, Elizabeth Dafter of Richard and Martha Arnalld.
—.	3.	1683.	Arnald, Richard departed ye Boddy.
17.	2.	1686	Coale, William s. of Wm. and Eliz. the Rellicke of Gorg Skipw th.
28.	3.	1683.	Chew, Samuell s. of Samuell and Ann.
2.	5.	1686	Chew, Ann d. of Samuell and Ann.
8.	2.	1687.	Chew, John s. of Samuell and Ann.
1.	5.	1679	Harrison, Samuel s. of Richard & Elizabeth, of Carroll County.

ii

Day.	Month.	Year.	
27.	12.	1680	Harrison, Sarah d. of Richard & Elizabeth
27.	8.	1682.	Harrison, Elizabeth d. of Richard & Elizabeth.
10.	8.	1864	Harrison, Mary d. of Richard & Elizabeth.
			maryed to Samuell Chew and d. t. l. 4. 6. 1725
3.	12.	1686	Harrison, Richard s. of Richard and Elizabeth.
14.	10.	1688	Harrison, Elizabeth d. of Richard and Elizabeth d. t. l.
6.	1.	1693	Harrison, Elizabeth wife to Richard of Calvert County d. h. n. l. "being delivered of A boy 27. 12 mo. 1693 wch. said boy his Life was spent before born Into the world wch. was named Josiah"
23.	5.	16—	Hannah of Edward & Mary Sarson.
12.	8.	168–	Eliz: Sarson.
17.	8.	1683	Birckhead, Nehemiah s. of Nehemiah & Elizabeth of annarundell County.
10.	6.	1685	Birckhead, Margaret d. of Nehemiah & Elizabeth of annarundell County.
16.	8.	1682.	Galloway, Sam ll: s. of Sam ll: & Sarah of Anarndel County
			Galloway, Hanna Dafter of Sam ll: & Sarah was borne.
25.	11.	1685	Galloway, Sarah Deceased.
5.	11.	1689	Galloway, Rich d s. of Sam ll & Ann, "Deseste ye 16 of the 8 mo 89."
		1691	Galloway, Peter s. of Sam ll: & Ann, & "Desest at 7 weak ould"
14.	11.	1692	Galloway, Jo n s. of Sam ll: & Aun, "Desest at 10 mo. & 2 weakes ould".
6.	12.	1693.	Galloway, Jo n s. of Sam ll. & Ann.
11.	2	1695	Galloway, Ann Dafter of Sam ll. & Ann.
18.	10.	1683	Skipwith, Gorg of Annarndell County D. t. L.
1.	10.	1684	Skipwith, Elizebeth Dafter of Gorg & Elizebeth Desest.
10.	12.	1694	Skipwith, Gorg s. of Gorg & Elizabeth Desest.
11.	7.	1687	Coale, William s. of William & Eliz: Desest.
2.	9.	1697	Richardson, William D. H. N. L.
15.	5.	1689	Wm. Richardson & Marget Smith, was Mareyed.

Day. Month. Year.

1.	(5)	1690.	Richardson, Wm. s. of Wm. & Marget
			and Dyed the 22d of 12 mo. 1731–2
31.	5.	169(2)	Richardson, Elizabeth d. of Wm. & Marget.
14.	3.	1694	Richardson, Samuell s. of Wm. & Marget,
			and D. H. N. L. 16th of 8 mo. 1697.
7.	3.	1096	Richardson, Sophia d. of Wm & Marget.
26.	—.	1698	Richardson, Sarah d. of Wm. & Marget.
31.	11.	1700–1	Richardson, Joseph s. of Wm. & Marget.

1.	11.	1703–4	Richardson, Elizerbeth Senr. D. H. N. L.
13.	7.	1703	Richardson, Samuell s. of Wm. & Margtt.
25.	10.	170(5)	Richardson, Daniell s of Wm. & Margrete.
			and D. i. n. L. 9th 8 mo. 1756.
—.	12.	17—.	Richardson, Rich d s. of Wm. & Margett.
—	4.	——	Richardson, Nathan s. of Wm. & Margtt.
20.	9.	1715	Richardson, Thomas s. of Wm. & Margarrett.
24.	2.	1722	Richardson, Sam ll above mentioned, D. t. L.

N. B. The remaining fourth part of this leaf has been cut off with a knife; it contained at least one entry.

30.	7.	1692.	Richardson, John, first Sonne of Daniell & Elizabeth
			Dyed Aboute 4 months after.
22.	11.	1693	Richardson, Leurania d. of Dan ll & Eliz: of Anna-rundle County.
3.	1.	1695–6	Richardson, Daniell s. of Dan ll & Eliz:
7.	1.	1697–8	Richardson, John s. of Dan ll & Eliz:
12.	2.	17(2)2	Richardson, John above mentioned, d. t. L.

15.	2.	1688	Thomas, Sam ell & Marey Hucthins maryed.
31.	1.	1689.	Thomas, Sarah of Sam ll & Marey, of annarundle County.
1.	12.	1690.	Thomas, Samell sone of ye abovesaid.
11.	1.	1693	Thomas, Samuell the 2d sone of ye aboves d.
1.	1.	1694	Thomas, Phillip sone to ye above Said.
15.	2.	1697	Thomas, sone to Samell and Mary.
28.	10.	1698	Thomas, Elizabth Daughtter unto Sam ell & Marey.
6.	9.	170(0)	Thomas, Marey Daughter un to Sam ell & Mary.
12.	9.	1702	Thomas, Samuell ye 3th; and D. t l. 3th of 2d mo. 17(76.) The last two figures are written over, "80," the true date.

iv

27.	11.	17(24)	The above Sarah after living with Her Husband Joseph Richardson between Ninetean & twenty years D. H. N. L. Joseph Richardson that was Husband to the above
18.	6.	1748	Sarah, D. h. N. L. in Seventy-first year of his age.

14.	10.	1704.	Robertson, s. Samuell of Danll & Sarah.
28.	10.	1705.	Robertson, Elizabeth d. of Danll & Sarah.
27.	7.	1708.	Robertson, Sarah d. of Danll & Sarah.
18.	9.	168–.	Waters, Mary d. of John & Elizabeth.
21.	8.	1689.	Watters, Eliz : d. of John & Elizabeth.
3.	3.	1699.	" " d. t. L.

29.	12.	1692.	Watters, Margrat Daught. of John & Elizabeth.
10.	5.	1696.	Watters, John s. of John & Elizabeth.
14.	5.	1699.	Watters, Wm. s. of John & Elizabeth.
8.	10.	1702.	Watters, Joseph s. of John & Elizabeth.
			Departed is life In the twluth month December 1764
9.	6.	1769	Webster, Mary D. t L.

16.	1.	1703	Hopkins, Eliz : d. of Gerrard & Margaret.
2.	9.	1706	Hopkins, Joseph s. of Gerrrard & Margaret.
7.	1.	1709	Hopkins, Gerrard s.
9.	1.	1711	Hopkins, Phillip s.
16.	11.	1713	Hopkins, Sam ll s.
15.	10.	1715	Hopkins, Richard s.
8.	6.	1718	Hopkins, William s.
30.	8.	1720	Hopkins, Johns. s.
27.	2.	1772	Hill, Elizabeth D. h. n. l. aged 69 years.
3.	7.	1777	Hopkins, Gerrard s. of Gerrard & Margrett, deceased aged 68.

21.	2.	1708	Talbott, Cassandra d. of John & Mary.
3.	7.	1777	Hopkins, Gerrard of Gerrard & Margrett D. T. L. after a Tedouss disorder aged 68.

8.	10.	1702	Lawrence, Eliza of Benja: & Rachell.
27.	11.	1704	Lawrence, Benja. s. of Benja: & Rachell.
2.	4.	1707	Lawrence, Sophia, Dar of Benja: & Rachell.
11.	9.	1709	Lawrence, John s of Benja: & Rachell.

| 6.. | 1. | 1711 | Lawrence, Levin s. of Benja: & Rachell. |
| 11. | 11. | 1716 | Lawrence, Margrett d. of Benja: & Rachell. |

The Ages of ye children of Wm. & Eliza Coale:

3.	10.	1692	Coale, Eliza.
24.	10.	1694	Coale, Mary.
11.	2.	1697	Coale, Wm.
14.	5.	1699	Coale, Hannah.
24.	6.	1701	Coale, Sam l.
5.	8.	1703	Coale, Priscilla.
28.	1.	1705	Coale, Thomas.
25.	12.	1706–7	Coale, Sarah.
10.	6.	1709	Coale, Ann.

11.	11.	1705	Miles, Sarah d. of Thomas & Ruth.
5.	11.	1707	Miles, Thomas s. of Thomas & Ruth.
3.	7.	1710	Miles, Elizabeth d.of Thomas & Ruth.
15.	1.	1710–11	Miles, Ruth, mother of the aboves d children deceased.
10.	9.	1710	Hanson, Jonathan s. to Jonathan & Kezia
3.	4.	1719	Hanson, Margrett d. to Jonathan & Mary.
?.	6.	1721	Hanson, Margrett Died
19.	12.	1720	Hanson, Mary d. of the afsd. Jonathan & Mary.
10.	4.	1723	Hanson, Mordaca s. of Jona. & Mary.

6.	5.	1706	Richardson, Sam ll s· of Joseph & Sarah.
19.	7.	1708	Richardson, Joseph, the 2d s. of Joseph & Sarah.
13.	7.	1710	Richardson, Maey d. of Joseph & Sarah.
26.	10.	1712	Richardson, Willm: 3d s. of Joseph & Sarah.
29.	1.	1716	Richardson, Phillip 4th s. of Joscph & Sarah.
18.	1.	1716–17	Richardson, Elizabeth, 2d d. of Joseph & Sarah.
3.	3.	1719	Richardson, Sarah, 3d d. of Joseph & Sarah.
19.	1.	1720–21	Richardson, John s. of Joseph & Sarah.
5.	3.	1723	Richardson, Richard, s. of Joseph & Sarah.
22.	7.	1736	The above said Richd Richardson D. t. L. at his Bro. Thomas Coale at Bush River and was buryed at the buring place on the plantion of John Crokett Late of Bush River in baltemore Co.

9.	3.	1718	Hill, Priscilla d. of Henry & Mary.

Coale, Mary, Wife of Thomas & d. of Joseph & Sarah Richardson, D. t. L. and was buryed at the burying place: on the Plantation of John Crockett Late of Bush River in Baltemore County.

25.	11.	1714.	Birckhead, Joseph s. of Nehemiah & Margarett.
22.	1.	1715.	Birckhead, Margaret d. of Nehemiah & Margaret.
11.	1.	1719–20	Birckhead, Nehemiah the father of the abovesd. Children D. t. L.
3.	11.	1739–40	Birckhead, Joseph d. t. L. on the sixth day of the Weak aged Twenty five years wanting a few Days.

11.	1.	1706	Hawkings, Aaron s. of Thomas & Elizabeth
19.	4.	1708	Hawkings, Joseph s. of Thomas & Elizabeth.
7.	11.	1713–14	Hawkings, Ruth. d. of Thomas & Elizabeth.

2.	4.	1705	Moore, Deborah d. of Mordai. & Deborah. at South River in Maryland
18.	8.	1706	Moore, Hannah. d. of Mordai. & Deborah. Deceased 26 & Buryed 27 by her Brother and Sister Mordai: & Elizh. att West River Burying place in Maryland.
29.	6.	——	Moore, Mary d. of Mordai. & Deborah att the house of our dear Brother and Sister Hill att Philada, Penselvania.
30.	6.	1710	Moore, Hesther d. of Mordai & Deborah att South River in Maryland.
11.	8.	1712	Moore, Elizabeth d. of Mordai & Deborah at South River in Maryland.
1.	10.	1718	Moore, Elizabeth was buryed att West River Burying Place In Maryland.
4.	8.	1714	Moore, Rachel d. of Mordai & Deborah, at South River in Mary

13.	2.	1720	Galloway, Samuell s. of Richard & Hannah D. t. L. at London, and was buried there in friends beuring Ground in bun field.

vii

20.	1.	1722	Galloway, Ann widow of the abovsed Samuell Deceased
28.	12.	1730–1	Galloway, Richard son of the abovsed Samuell deceased.
14.	Dec.	1737	Sprigg, Thomas was maried to Elisabeth dau. of Richard & Sophia Galloway.
29.	Dec.	1781	Sprigg, Thomas Departed is natural Life, aged about 67 years last November and was buried in is garding.

16.	11.	1721	Galloway, Elizabeth d. of Richard & Sophia.
16.	Dec.	1739	Sprigg, Richard s. of Thomas & Elizabeth.
21.	4.	1766	Sprigg, Sophia d. of Richard & Margrett.
6.	Oct.	1767	Sprigg, Rebekah d. of Richard & Margrett.
25.	Aug.	1770	Sprigg, Elizabeth d. of Richard & Margrett.
15.	Apr.	1772	Sprigg, Margrett d of Richard & Margrett & deceased about three month after
2.	July.	1775	Sprigg, Henrietta Sarah d. of Richard & Margrett,
14.	Feb.	1779	Sprigg, Margrett d. of Richard & Margrett.

28.	11.	1663	Galloway, Richard, Son.
28.	8.	1736	Galloway, Richard, Sen. D. t. L. and was beuryed at West River Meeting Grave Yard
26.	6.	1668	Richardson, William Sr s. of William & Elizabeth
13.	5.	1744	Richardson, William Departed this Life buryed ye 15.
14.	4.	1745	Richardson, Thomas s. of William & Margaret, D. t. L. at his house on the Eastern Shore in Kent County

6.	2.	1732	Richardson, Samll s. of Richard & Margrett.
9.	4.	1735	Richardson, Sophia Daughter of Dito.

7.	9.	1736	Richardson, William s. of Nathan & Elizabeth.

8.	8.	1732	Cowman, Joseph s. of Joseph & Sarah.
1.	8.	1733	Cowman, Ann d. of Joseph & Sarah.
24.	12.	1735	Cowman, Mary, d of Joseph & Sarah.
24.	4.	1737	Cowman, John, d. of Joseph & Sarah.
5.	4.	1737	Hopkins, Gerrard s. of Philip & Eliza.
7.	11.	1738–9	Hopkins, Richd second s. of Philip & Eliza.
23.	11.	1740–41	Hopkins, Eliza, d. of Philip & Eliza.
25.	10.	1742–3	Hopkins, Phillip the 3 s. carryd. over

(to back of following page.)

| 16. | 5. | 1745 | Hopkins, Samuel |
| 29. | 10. | 1746 | Birckhead, Nehemiah, of John & Christain. |

7.	9.	1735	Richardsón, William s of Nathan & Elizabeth..
26.	10.	1740	Richardson, Elizabeth d. of Nathan & Elizabeth.
26.	6.	1744	Richardson, Nathan s. to Nathan & Elizabeth.
10.	5.	1746	Richardson, Eliza. wife of Nathan D. h. L. and was Buryed at Bush River at the Buriall Place of her father John Crockett Late of Baltemor County.
12.	June.	1725	Thomas, Samuel s. of Philip & Ann.
3.	July.	1727	Thomas, Philip.
1	Jan.	1731	Thomas, Mary.
8	Mar.	1732–3	Thomas, Eliza.
17.	July.	1736	Thomas, Richard.
26.	Aug.	1743	Thomas, John.
23.	Aug.	1777	Thomas, John, the above, was married to Sarah Murray.
6.	July.	1778	Thomas, Ann their daughter
29.	July.	1782	Thomas, Philip s. of John & Sarah.

14.	11.	1740	Moore, Margaret the first child of Mordai. & Eliz. at her Father's House Near London Town in Maryland.
13.	9.	1743	Moore, Mary the second child Ditto.
2.	8.	1745	Moore, Richard third child Ditto.
10.	7.	1747	Moore, Samuel Preston fourth child Ditto..

1.	12	1749–50	Richardson, Daniell s of Nathan & Hanah:
16.	3.	1806	Thomas, Margret Wife to John D. t. l.
19.	8.	1794	Brooke, Elizababeth wife to Basel D. t. L.
22.	8.	1794	Brooke, Basel Departed this Life, a few minits after Sun Set.
5.	7.	1750	Galloway, Ann d. of Joseph & Ann
27.	11.	1756	Thomas, Philip s. of Philip Juner & Ann Juner..
21.	6.	1758	Thomas, Ann d.
4	7.	1760	Thomas, Ann d. of Philip Juner & Ann Juner D. t. L.

| 31. | 11. | 1731 | Hopkins, Margret d. of Garrard & Mary. "Last day of ye 11 mo. January in ould Stile." |
| 25. | 6. | 1732 | Hopkins, Garrard. |

ix

11.	9.	1734	Hopkins, Mary d. of ye above Garrard & Mary.
20	7.	1737	Hopkins, Sarah.
7.	12.	1739	Hopkins, Richard the Second son of Garrard & Mary, and died soon after and was buried at West river buring ground.
3.	9.	1741	Hopkins, Elizabeth
30.	10.	1742	Hopkins, Rachel.
11.	11.	1744	Hopkins, Joseph.
20.	1.	1747	Hopkins, Richard.
29.	6.	1749	Hopkins, Hannah.
15.	10.	1752	Hopkins, Elisha.
11.	3.	1747	Hopkins, Ezekiel s. of Johns and is wife Mary.
8.	5.	1751	Hopkins, Johns s. of Johns and Mary.
3.	2.	1759	Hopkins, Samuel s. of Johns & Elizabeth.
24.	9.	1760	Hopkins, Philip s of Johns & Elizabeth.

"Carried over the other side."

14.	9.	1756	Richardson, Elizabith d. of Richard & Elizabeth.
8.	1.	1758	Richardson, Richard s of Richard & Elizabeth.
17.	1.	1775	Richardson, Richard Departed is natural.
20.	4.	1760	Richardson, Mary d. of Richard & Elizabeth.
5.	2.	1763	Richardson, Ann Thomas d. of Richard & Elizabeth.
28.	5.	1765	Richardson, John Thomas s. of Richard & Elizabeth.
12	Aug.	1767	Richardson, William s of Richard & Elizabeth. Richardson, Joseph s. of Richard & Elizabeth. Richardson, Rebekah d. of Richard & Elizabeth.
24.	9	1744	Richardson, Joseph s. of William & Ann.
27.	7.	1747	Richardson, Ann d. of William & Ann.

"September in old stile."

2.	3.	1762	Hopkins, Richard s. of Johns & Elizabeth.
7.	1.	1764	Hopkins, Mary d of Johns & Elizabeth.
20.	2.	1766	Hopkins, Margrit d. of Johns & Elizabeth.

17.	1.	1755	Cowman, Richard s. of Joseph & Elizabeth.
13.	Apl.	1757	Cowman, Joseph the second son of Joseph & Elizabeth.
1.	7.	1759	Cowman, Elizabeth d. of Joseph & Elizabeth.
26.	7.	1762	Cowman, Samuel.
30.	3.	1765	Cowman, John.
16.	11.	1769	Cowman, Sarah d. of Joseph & Elizabeth.

Day.	Month.	Year.	
24.	10.	1769	Hopkins, Garrard s. of Johns & Elizabeth.
			Hopkins, Elizabeth d. of Johns & Elizabeth.
30.	Nov.	1772	Hopkins, Evan s. of Johns & Elizabeth.
26.	Feb.	1775	Hopkins, Ann d. of Johns & Elizabeth.
7.	Sept.	1777	Hopkins, Rachel. d. of Johns & Elizabeth.

in	Feb.	1755	Hill, Sarah Senr. D. h. n. L. in the 83 year of her age.
in	Feb.	1756	Richardson, Margrett D. h. n. L. in the 84 year of her age
11.	Jan.	1761	Hill, Sarah wife of Joseph D. h. n. l.
	Aug.	1756	Richardson, Daniel D. h. n. L.
in		1760	Richardson, Margrett wife of Richard D. h. n. l.
25.	2.	1761	Richardson, Richard Deceased.
25	10.	1761	Hill, Joseph D. h. n. l. aged near 56 years.
27.	1.	1781	Galloway, Sophia D. h. n. L. in her 85 year of her age.

5.	11.	1744	Gover, Ephriam s. of Robert & Sarah.
28.	1.	1745	Gover, Sarah d. of Robert & Sarah.
25.	6.	1746	Gover, Mary d. of Robert & Sarah.
14.	3.	1747	Gover, Rachel d. of Robert & Sarah.
10.	10	1748	Gover, Ephriam s. of Robert & Sarah.
5	8.	1750	Gover, Hannah d. of Robert & Sarah.
18.	2.	1752	Gover, William s. of Robert & Sarah.
17	10.	1753	Gover, Robert s. of Robert & Sarah.
3.	3.	1755	Gover, Jean d. of Robert & Sarah.
23.	3.	1757	Gover, Margret d. of Robert & Sarah.
22.	9	1759	Gover, Elizabeth d. of Robert & Sarah.

9.	8	1758	Cowman, Joseph s. of John & Sarah.
18.	4.	1760	Cowman, Mary d. of John & Sarah.
6.	6.	1762	Cowman, Garrard s. of John & Sarah.
18.	4.	1764	Cowman, John s. of Do.
9.	2.	1766	Cowman, Sarah d. of Do.
22.	5.	1769	Cowman, Margrett d. of Ditto.
24.	7.	1771	Cowman, Ann d. of Ditto.
12.	3.	1774	Cowman, Elizabeth d. of Ditto.
13.	9.	1777	Cowman, Richard s. of Ditto.

In	May.	1750	Hill, Joseph Jun first child of Henry & Mary at West River.

24.	12.	1751	Hill, Henrietta d. of Henry & Mary ("Decr.") at the same place.
23.	11.	1762	Thomas, Philip s. of Samuel & Mary dec. aged 68 years.
22.	5.	1777	Thomas, Ann widow of above Philip D. h. n. L. in the 71st year of her age.
23.		1766	Harris, Margrett, the beloved wife of William and mother of this family, Departed this life the 23th day of the month and was buried in friends Buriel place near the Clifts the 7th of the same month being in the 56 year of her age.
26.	3.	1772	Harris, William s. of Samuel & Rachel.
17.	9.	1774	Harris, Samuel s. of Samuel & Rachel.

The ages of the Children of Samuel & Sarah

10.	3.	1725	Plummer, Ruth.
8.	7.	1726	Plummer, Thomas.
3.	5.	1728	Plummer, Joseph
30.	8.	1730	Plummer, Samuel.
3.	1.	1731–2	Plummer, Casander.
30.	6	1734	Plummer, Sarah.
16.	5.	1736	Plummer, Abraham.
16.	12.	1738	Plummer, Rachel.
16.	1.	1742	Plummer, Ursula.
29.	3.	1744	Plummer, Elizabeth.
26.	8	1747	Plummer, Anna.
16.	10.	1751	Plummer, Suhanah.
20.	5.	1764	Garritson, John Hutchinson s. of Cornelus & Priscilla.
8.	9.	1765	Garritson, Thomas s. of Cornelus & Priscilla.

5.	5.	1766	Brooke, Jemes s. of Basil & Elizabeth.

19.	9.	1770	Hopkins Isaac Howell
19.	12.	1770	Hopkins Isaac Howell s. of Joseph & Elizabeth.
			(Above two entries crossed out.)
6.	1.	1772	Robertson, Ann d of William & Elizabeth.
9.	5.	1774	Robertson, Samuel s. of William & Elizabeth.

30.	Dec.	1722	Richdson William s. of Jose. & Rebekah.
24.	July.	1725	Richardson, Richd. s. of Jose. & Rebekah.

Day.	Month.	Year.	
5.	Mar.	1727	Richardson, Mary. d. of Jose. & Rebekah.
27.	12.	1779	Hopkins, Jushua s. of Johns & Cattey of Philidelphia
16.	8.	1782	Hopkins, Joseph s. Johns & Catty.
20.	5.	1777	Thomas, Ann d. of Samuel Chew & Mary is wife dec. and buried at west river Grave Yard.
31.	3.	1781	Hopkins, Isaac Howell s. of Elisha & Hannah.
18.	7.	1782	Hopkins, Deborah d. of Elisha & Hannah.
12.	3.	1781	Hance, Samuel s. of Benjamin & Sarah.
27.	9.	1782	Hance, Thomas Cliverly s. of Benjamin & Sarah.
7.	6,	1784	Hance, Ann d. of Benjamin & Sarah.

The Names & Agis of Gidion & Elizabeth Dare's children.

9.	2.	1776	Dare, Sarah.
17.	9.	1777	Dare, Priscilla.
28.	10.	1779	Deare, Thomas, Cleaverly.
18.	10.	1781	Dare, Henry.
6.	9.	1783	Dare, Eliz:th.
8.	3.	1786	Dare, Gidion.
18.	12.	1787	Dare, William.

The Agis of John & Johannah Plummer Childrin

3.	1.	1774	Plummer, Jerom s. of the Above
7.	9.	1775	Plummer, Gerrard s. of the Above
13.	3.	1777	Plummer, Mary d. of John & Johanna.
12.	1.	1779	Plummer, Ann Thomas d. of John & Johanna.
20.	4.	1781	Plummer, John s. of John & Johanna.
4.	10.	1783	Plummer, Joseph s. of John & Johanna.

The ages of Richd. Thomas Junr. & Deborah's children.

1.	8.	1784	Thomas, Elizabeth.
27.	9.	1788	Thomas, Frederick Augustus.
18.	10.	1791	Thomas, Mary.
26.	4.	1794	Thomas, Sarah.

The Ages of the Children of Bernard Gilpin & Sarah his wife

30.	5.	1794	Gilpin, Sarah.
21.	11.	1795	Gilpin, Elizabeth.

Day.	Month.	Year.	
1.	7.	1797	Gilpin, Ann Robinson.
10.	2.	1799	Gilpin, Thomas.
20.	3.	1801	Gilpin, Samuel.
20.	5.	1803	Gilpin, Hannah.
16.	4.	1805	Gilpin, Lydia
			The Ages of the children of Bernard & Latitia Gilpin
10.	8.	1808	Gilpin, William Henry
12.	4.	1810	Gilpin, Joshua Canby

19.	12.	1770	Hopkins, Isaac Howell s. of Joseph & Elizabith
5.	11.	1771	Hopkins, Patience d. of Joseph & Elizabith
22.	1.	1775	Hopkins, Gerrard s. Joseph & Elizabith
18.	4.	1777	Hopkins, Hanner & Mary Twins d. of Joseph & Elizabith
10.	3.	1781	Hopkins, Joseph & Elizabeth Twins s. & d. of Joseph & Elizabith
16.	6.	1783	Hopkins, Isaac Gray s. of Joseph & Elizabith
24.	10.	1785	Hopkins, Prisciljah d. of Joseph & Elizabith
9.	4.	1788	Hopkins, Mary d. of Joseph & Elizabith
9.	4.	1790	Hopkins, Samuel s. of Joseph & Elizabith
3.	8.	1792	Hopkins, Sarah d. of Joseph & Elizabith
2.	3.	1779	Hopkins, Margarett d. of Joseph & Elizabith

8.	10.	1792	Snowden, Elizabith d. of Philip & patience.
13.	1	1794	Snowden, Saml. s. of Philip & patience.

			The Ages of the Children of Thomas Norris & Ann his Wife.
4.	10.	1793	Norris, Mary Ann.
30.	4.	1795	Robert.
14.	10.	1796	John.
.31.	1.	1799	Sarah.
13.	2.	1802	Elizabeth.
			(A leaf torn out, probably blank.)
			The Age of the Child of Samuel Lukens and Hannah his Wife
14.	1.	1804	Lukens, Elizabeth.
			The ages of the children of Joseph & Susanna Plummer.
12.	3.	1807	Plummer, John Thomas.
20.	2.	1809	Mary Mifflin.
			(16 blank leaves, and one torn out.)

Elliott, John s. of Samuel & is wife Mary.

(Above entry crossed out.)

12. Nov. 1780   Elliott, Samuel was md. to Mary dau. of Richard & Elizabeth Richardson at West River

2   Nov. 1781   Elliott, John s. of Saml & Mary.

27.   5   1782   Richardson, Elizabeth D. h. N L.

4. ' 11.   Richardson, Joseph s. of William & Margret d. t. l. Aged 81 years was interd in Johns Hopkins Burying Ground by his daughter at South River in the year of our Lord 1782

14.   9.   1756–7 Richardson, Eliza. d. of Richd. & Eliza.

20.   Mar. 1762   and d. t. l.

8.   1.   1758   Richardson, Richd. s. to the Above.

17.   Jan. 1775   and d. t. l. in ye 16 year of his Age.

20.   4.   1760   Richardson, Mary d to ye Above.

5.   2.   1763   Richdson, Ann Thomas d to ye Above.

25.   5.   1765.   Richdson, Jno. Thomas.

14.   8.   1767.   Richardson, Willm.

17. ' 7.   1770.   Richardson, Jose.

26.   8.   1772.   Richardson, Rebeckah.

11.   8.   1775   Richardson, Deborah Snowden.

29.   8.   1808   Bentley, Mary. (I think this is an entry of death) Brookeville

Bentley, Caleb

Bentley, H.

(The remaining 15 leaves have been used "for Entering of frends Epestles & papers.")

All the Lawrence Marriages Births, and Deaths, from the First
Record Book of New York Friends' Meeting; copied by L. B. T

Day.	Month.	Year.	
9.	8.	1746	Hannah Lawrence, of Flushing md Moses Mullenux (signed "Mullenex") of West Chester
7.	6.	1754	Caleb Lawrence md. Sarah dau. of James dec^d and Elizabeth Burling at Flushing.

Children of Richard and Hannah Lawrence of Flushing.

3.	2.	1718	Mary
15.	4.	1719	Elizabeth
10.	9.	1721	Joseph
1.	15.	172$\frac{3}{4}$	Caleb
2.	2.	1726	Hannah
29.	7.	1728	Liddya
31.	11.	1730-31	John, and lived but 9 days
22.	11.	1731-2	John
11.	12.	1734-5.	Efingham
6.	11.	1737	Joseph Larance
			Norriss Lawrence
23.	10.	1743	Ann wife of Norriss Lawrence born.

Steven and Amy Lawrence of Flushing

7.	3.	1735	Summerset
7.	4.	1737	Lanselott
3.	6.	1739	Deborah
17.	7.	1741	Lennerd

Children of Norriss and Ann Lawrence

9.	10.	1765	Mary
21.	9.	1767	Hannah
15.	2.	1769	Norris

Children of John and Ann Lawrence

13.	6.	1756	Edward Burling
8.	7.	1758	Hannah
6.	6.	1760	Effingham
11.	9.	1762	Mary
17.	10.	1763	Mary
15.	5.	1765	Catherine
2.	9.	1768	Jane
24	12.	1770	Phebe

Day. Month. Year.

22	5.	1772	Anna
21.	10.	1774	John Burling
17.	3.	1778	Phebe and Cornelia, twins
14	9.	1740	Phebe wife of Joseph Lawrence born.
12.	5	1775	Hester dau. of Caleb and Sarah Lawrence born.

Children of Richard and Hannah Lawrence

28.	12.	1700	Ann
25.	2.	1791	Henry Haydock.
17.	4.	1776	Mary Widdo of Samuel Lawrence of Black Stump deceased.
30.	9.	1732	Obadiah Lawrence, a Minister d.

Lawrence burials from the records of Christ Church, Philadelphia, between 1709 and 1760 extracted by C. R. Hildeburn Esq.

Nov.	24	1722	Laurence, ———.
Apl	23. .	1723	Laurence, Mary.
July.	25.	1723	Laurence, John son of Thomas, *Gent.*
Dec.	2.	1728	Laurence. Longfield son of Thomas, Esq.
Jan.	15.	1728-9	Laurence, Catherine dau. of Thomas, Esq.
Nov.	1.	1731	Laurence, Longfield son of Thomas, Esq.
Apl.	22.	1754	Lawrence, Thomas, Esq.
Sept.	8.	1756	Lawrence. Robert Hunter son of Thomas
Oct.	29.	1756	Lawrence, Francis
Nov.	15.	1756	Lawrence, ——— son of Thomas.
Apl.	1.	1746	Wilmorth wife of Gyles Larrence.

ARMS OF RUTHERFURD.

Nov.		1879	Canby, Edwin Knight md Mae Blackman.
Nov.	9.	1880	Canby, Edwin Knight d.
Aug.	21.	1878	Canby, Samuel d.
July	11.	1882	Carroll, Harry D G. d.
July	2.	1873	Carter, Rev. Frederick B md. Fanny dau. of John W. Lawrence.
May	10.	1874.	Gertrude May their dau b,
Nov.	12.	1876.	Mary Lawrence their dau. b.
June	3.	1878.	Louise their dau. b.
		1881	Cheston Galloway d.
May	15.	1881.	Chew, Minnie West dau. of Samuel Claggett and wife of Rev. John H.
July	31.	1878.	Chew, Benjamin, s. of Samuel of Cliveden b.
May	24.	1880.	Chew, Oswald s. of Samuel of Cliveden b.
Oct.	12.	1880	Early, Hallie R. md. William Van Wyck
Sept.	4.	1878	Ellicott, Evan T. md. Alice Stella McCormick.
June	20.	1879	Ellicott, Gilmor Meredith, their son b.
June	14.	1881	Ellicott, Harvey M. (Bond) Widow of Evan T. d.
Dec.	26.	1876	Ellicott, James P. s. of Thomas P. and Catherine (Allen) b.
Nov.	3.	1880	Ellicott, Samuel d.
			Children of William & Ann S. P. (Chew) Grason.
Sept.	3.	1876.	Mary Chew b.
May	13.	1878.	Elizabeth Ridgely b.
Dec.	21.	1879.	Andrew Sterrett Ridgely, b.
			Children of J. Alex and Elizabeth A. (Chew) Green.
Dec.	10.	1878	Charles Ridgely b
July.	18.	1880	I. Milton b.
Oct.	5.	1881.	Bessie Chew b.
May,	27.	1881	Hopkins, William d
May	13.	1869	Jolliffe, Lizzie H. md Nathaniel B. Crenshaw, and had issue :
Mch.	5.	1870.	Nathaniel B. b.
Mch	24.	1871	Nathaniel B. d.
July	3.	1871	John M. b.
Aug.	14.	1875	John M. d.
July	6.	1874	Margaret J. b.

Feb. 18. 1880. Fanny G. b.

Apl.	15.	1879	Jolliffe, Fanny M. md. William Gilmor.
Jany.	20.	1881	Knight, Dr. Samuel T. d.
Oct.	15.	1880	Knight, Eliza Snowden. d.
Oct.	8.	1880	Knight, Ann Rebecca d.
Apl.	25.	1882	Lawrence, Susan Newbold md James W. Walsh Jr.
Jany.		1882	Lewis, Thomas Chew d.
		1876	Lyman. Mary Kerr Coffey dau. of Charles H. and Rebecca (Chew) b.
		1880	Lyman, Frisby Freeland son. of the same b.
Aug.	5.	1867	Montgomery, John C. d.
Nov.	28.	1880	Morris, Ann (Cheston) wife of Dr. Caspar d.
Nov.	5.	1879	Morris, Effingham B md. Ellen Douglas dau. of H. Nelson Burroughs and has issue :
Nov.		1880.	Rhoda b.
Feby.	8.	1879	Newlin, Thomas S d.
July	3.	1881	Pemberton, Gen. John C. d
Feby.	6.	1881	Peterson, J. Howard, drowned.
Sept.	3.	1841.	Philips, Sophia (Chew) wife of Henry d.
Sept.	25,	1832.	Poultney, Thomas Jr. d.
Apl.	22.	1880	Reese, Walter d.
		1880	Smith, Harriet J. dau. of Thomas and Elizabeth (Leiper) Md. William De Forest
Oct.		1882	Thomas, Ann (Sewall) widow of Thomas S. d.
Apl.	18.	1881	Thomas, Ann (Gray) widow of George Gray d.
Oct.	11.	1882	Thomas, Rev. Lawrence Buckley was md. to Mary Berry dau. of Thomas Farrell and Marion L. (Berry) McCobb at the Church of the Reformation Brooklyn N. Y. by Rev. D. V. M. Johnson D. D. assisted by the Rev. John G. Bacchus.
Oct.		1860.	Todhunter, Eliza wife of Joseph d.
July	3.	1881	Upton, Mrs. Sarah dau. of Peter Thomson d.
June	17.	1878	Wethered, Samuel d.
			Children of Dr. Randolph and Rebecca Fayssoux (Leiper) Winslow
Nov	17.	1878	Nathan b.
Mch.	7.	1880	John Leiper b.
July	2.	1881	Fitz Randolph b.

ARMS OF GEORGE.

Signatures,

From Marriage Certificate
of Samuel Thomas
and Mary Snowdon,
August 11th 1730.

Traced Sept. 24th 1881.

Evan Thomas

Daniel Browne	Hannah Lofton	Henrietta Thomas	Ralph L. Tho...
Morgan Browne Jun	Mary Comeys	Mary Tyson	Elizabeth ...
Joseph Browne	Simon Meredith	Elizabeth Ellicott	
Bartle Wilkins	Thomas Mifflin	Rachel Mason	
J. Browne		Wm Tyson	
John Marlin	Mary Frew	Daniel Mifflin	Evan Thomas
Edw. Conney	William Frew		Evan Thomas Senr
	And. Ellicott	Maria Thomas	
	James Iddings	Samuel Thomas	Saml Simmonds
		Richard Thomas	Joseph Simmonds
	Bartle Frew	Rachel Hodges	Isaac Tyson
	Jacob Lamb	Rebecca Lamb	
	William Frew Jun	Rebecca Frew	Mary Thomas
	John Hodges	Susanna Yarnall	Rich. L. Thomas
		Ann Thomas	

iE.

39
91
80
83
84
87
25
93
24
20
24
24
99
01
05
40
64
61
51
48
60·
58·
55·
45·
55·
69
60
55
70
60
50·

ARMS OF FAIRFAX.

REFERENCE INDEX.

ERRATA.

On page 9, line 17, change 1747 to 1748.
"   " 11,   "   8, change 1781 to 1771.
"   " 22,   "   17, It was not Edward but his father John Lane
                ' Chew who resided at "Lombardy Poplar,"
               afterwards burned.
"   " 23,   "   31, William was 3d son of Samuel and Sarah
               (Lock) Chew.
"   " 33,   "   2, change "Lieutenant" to "Purser."
"   " 87,   "   34, change "busbahd" to "husband."
"   " 104,   "   27, Rys Griffith was never Knighted.
"   " 112,   "   31, change "Worcestor" to "Worcester."
"   " 112,   "   5, change "48" to "18."
"   " iv,   "   33, insert "John" after "Thomas."

ARMS OF BUCKLEY.